HIDE AND SEEK

HIDE AND SEEK

BY JACK KETCHUM

GAUNTLET PUBLICATIONS
■ 2007 ■

Interior Page design by **Dara Hoffman**

ISBN 1-887368-99-X
13 digit ISBN 9781887368995

Manufactured in the United States of America

FIRST EDITION

Gauntlet Publications
5307 Arroyo Street
Colorado Springs, CO 80922
United States of America
Phone: (719) 591-5566
email: info@gauntletpress.com
Website: www.gauntletpress.com

To Robert Bloch,
for bothering with kids.

Acknowledgments

My thanks to Al Weller, Lance and Ellen Crocker, Alan Morrison, Marjorie Shepatin, Phillip Caggiano, David and Julie Winn, Ellen Antoville, and especially to Paula White.

One

I don't believe in omens, but I think you can know when you're in trouble.

Follow me on this, even if it sounds like bullshit.

I was working the stacks of two-by-four furring. What we needed was an eight-foot length off the top. We were nearly into the next bundle down but you could still see a couple of lengths left up there that didn't look too weathered, so I climbed up after one. I had my hands on one when the steel cable snapped on the bundle I was walking on. A sound like a whip cracking. Damn near took my head off too. And naturally I lost my footing. I fell ten feet to the tarmac in a shower of heavy lumber.

Not a scratch on me.

I was lucky.

But the boss gave me hell. You weren't supposed to go up there—though everybody did—you were supposed to use the forklift. There was an insurance problem. So I was breaking the rules.

That was the first thing. Getting damn near killed breaking the rules.

That same week I had the Chevy pickup out on the coast road, doing maybe sixty, when a big black tanker passed me on the downgrade. I let him have the highway. But then on the upgrade he slowed to a crawl. I swallowed diesel fumes behind him for a while and then pulled out to pass.

But I guess the guy wanted to play.

He wouldn't let me by. He'd move over across the broken yellow line just far enough so that there was a good chance of piling me into the hillside if I tried. Then he'd pull back again. Out and back. I could see him watching me through the rearview mirror.

It was very nasty.

I cursed him and waited for an opening.

It came on the downgrade again. By the time I saw it we were both of us doing seventy. Already that was hard on the pickup. My wheel would always wobble at sixty-five. So I held my breath and told myself to hell with it, you were only young once, and pressed it to eighty.

The pickup shook like it was trying to fall apart. I remembered the old bald tires. The downgrade was long and steep and we ran it neck and neck, he and I.

I passed him just as the road turned up again. I was sweating and my hands were trembling. I can see that bastard smiling at me as I passed him even to this day—not so much the man, but the wicked cut of the smile. A tanker is a very big thing on a narrow highway when it's running a foot and a half away from you at eighty for over a mile.

So that was the second thing. Being stupid and angry and taking bad risks. I could just as easily have waited him out. It had been a nice, sunny day.

~~~~~~~~~~

Then I stepped in dog shit.

Coming home from work, half a block from Harmon's.

Now, I know that's nothing. Meaningless. Silly. Even though it was a particularly big pile of dog shit, and fresh. But I'll tell you why I remember it and why I put it with the other things. It's very simple.

I wasn't looking where I was going.

Now, that's nothing either, unless you take into account the fact that it's completely contrary to my habits. I stare at the ground when I walk. I always do. I've been criticized for it now and then. My mother used to say I'd get nearsighted and stoop-shouldered. She lied, of course. I got tall and see at twenty-twenty.

But damn it, *I wasn't looking*.

I'm aware that these are all random events. And maybe it's just hindsight.

But sometimes it seems to me that once in a while you can look at all the random events you live through every day and see that suddenly there's a mechanism that's just clicked on, you can see it right then and there—and the events are not so random anymore. The mechanism is eating them, absorbing them, growing larger and larger, feeding on the events of your life. To what end? You don't know.

The mechanism is you.

But it's also fate, luck, chance. All the things that are *not* you but that will change you anyway, irreparably, forever.

Maybe you'd better forget all this.

I'm still a fool, and I meander.

TWO

BUT RIGHT AWAY SHE SCARED ME.

They all did, actually. All three of them. They were rich kids, for one thing, and I wasn't used to that.
~~~~~~~~~~

You should know right off that there was, and is, no more depressed county in the nation than Washington County. The per capita income is right up there with, say, Appalachia. Everyone I knew was barely scraping by. And here were these three rich kids popping around in Casey's fabulous old white '54 Chevy convertible or Steven's blue Chrysler Le Baron as though tired, sad old Dead River were Scarsdale or Beverly Hills. What in hell their folks were doing in this part of Maine at all I never could figure. Mount Desert, sure. But Dead River? I knew that the three families were friends back in Boston, and I guess it was somebody's idea of getting away from it all that brought them there. But I don't think the kids knew either.

They resented it, though. That was for sure. And I think resenting it made them crazy.

That was what really scared me.

All you had to do was look at them to see it. Casey most of all. You could see it in her eyes. Something caught in the act of throwing itself away, right there in front of you.

Recklessness. It scares me. It scares me today.

Because just writing this, that's a kind of recklessness too. It's going to bring it all back to me and I've kept it down nicely for a long time now. Not just what happened. But how I felt about Casey, how I feel about her still. I don't know which is worse, really, but I guess I'm going to find out.

Starting now.

I'll tell you how I knew she was crazy. It was the business with the car.

It was June, a Saturday or Sunday it must have been, because Rafferty and I were both off for the day. I remember it was unusually hot for that time of year, so we'd stopped at Harmon's for a six-pack and headed for the beach.

There's really only one good stretch of white sand around Dead River. The rest is either stone or gravel or else a sheer drop off slate cliffs nearly thirty feet to the sea. So on hot days just about everybody you know is there, and this was maybe the second or third good day that year, so naturally she was there too, way behind us by the cliffs, near the goat trail. The three of them were there.

We were hardly aware of them at first. Rafferty was a lot more interested in Lydia Davis, lying on a towel a few feet away. And I had my eye on a couple of tourist girls. Occasionally the wind would slide down off the cliffs and pull the music from their radio in our direction, but that was all. The beach was pretty crowded, and there was plenty to look at.

Then I saw this girl walk by me to test the water. Just a glimpse of her face as she passed.

The water was much too cold, of course. Not even the little kids were giving it a try. You wouldn't find much swimming here till late July or August. I watched her shiver and step backward when the first wave rolled over her feet. The black bikini was pretty spectacular. Somehow she'd already managed a good deep tan. From where I sat, I could see the goose bumps.

I watched her step forward. The water was up to her calves by then.

Rafferty was watching too. "More guts than brains," he said.

I mentioned that she was also beautiful.

"That too."

We watched her dive in.

The dive was clean and powerful. She came up facing us, spouting, long dark hair plastered smoothly back from the high, widow's peaked forehead.

I knew immediately she was not a native.

I remember her face looked so very naked just then, so clean and strong and healthy. She could not have been bred around here. Not around Dead River.

We're all of a type, you see. Or one of two.

We're all as poor and stunted and miserable as the scrub pines that struggle up through the thin hard cliffside soil. Or else—like Rafferty and me—you grew up long and lean as the runners that crept along the ground each spring and tried to strangle them. Either way, it showed.

But this girl showed you nothing. She was all smooth lines and breeding and a casual vigor. With skin most girls just dream of. Surfacing sleek as a seal, laughing. In water the temperature of which only a seal could love.

She opened her eyes. And that was another revelation.

They were such a shade of pale, pale blue that at first it was hard to see any color in them at all. Dead eyes, my brown-eyed father calls them. Depthless. Like the color of the sea when the sand is coral and the water's calm and shallow. Reflecting light, not absorbing it.

The cold must have been amazing. I watched her roll once through the water and turn to face us again. Just her head and neck showing. I could see her tremble, lips parted, blue eyes blinking, blind-seeming. The sun was warm on me, but I could almost feel the ache in her bones.

They say that very cold water can make a kind of ecstasy. But first there's pain.

I saw the face muscles contract and knew she had the pain.

I watched the drops of water roll down her body as she waded back to shore, sliding from muscle to muscle across the tight brown surface of skin. The bikini told you everything about her but the color of her pubic hair. Mostly it told you she was strong.

She walked right past me.

I kept watching. I saw her eyes flicker and move, and then she was gone up the beach to her friends. I thought she'd noticed me. And then I thought that that was wishful thinking.

I knew it wasn't Rafferty. Girls don't notice Rafferty. At twenty his face was still ravaged by pimples. His hands were stained with axle grease. His face was red with whiskey. It's not that I'm any great beauty, but my eyes are clear. I'm in pretty good shape to this day, and whatever small problem I've had with zits, I'd lost two years before, at eighteen. So maybe it was me.

I thought it was me.

And thinking that made something glad and constricting happen in my throat. A happy snake coiled there. I drank a beer, and it didn't go away.

~~~~~~~~~~

But it was rough just sitting there after that. I wanted to walk up the beach and talk to her in the worst way. But I was never any good at approaches.

Besides, I was way outclassed and I knew it.

I worked in a lumberyard.

I sold quarter-inch plywood and pine and two-by-twos to contractors and do-it-yourselfers.

College was on the back burner for a while and for all I cared it could fry there. Oh, I'd read a lot and my grades were okay, but I'd had it with school even worse than I'd had it with Dead River. Eventually that would change. But at the time I was content with three-fifty an hour and a little barmaid I knew called Lyssa Jean. Nice girl.

After that day on the beach, I never saw her again. Not once. Sorry, Lyssa Jean.

Anyhow, it was not much fun sitting there after that, but I stuck it out for another hour or so, hoping she'd get up for another swim. She didn't. In the meantime Rafferty had struck up a conversation with Lydia Davis.

Now that the tourists were in town Lydia was a lot more generally available. Off-season she was just about the prettiest thing we had in Dead River and you could buy her drinks all night long at the Caribou and hardly get a smile or a word out of her. She got nicer with competition around.

So I couldn't get Rafferty to leave. The dog in the honeypot. He kept baring his crooked teeth at her.

I quit trying.
~~~~~~~~~~

We had Rafferty's car that day but I figured I could probably hitch a ride along the coast road. I packed my gear, slipped on my jeans, shirt and sneakers and headed up the beach to the goat trail.

On the way I passed them. A tall, slim guy with dark skin and dark hair and a sharp, straight nose. And a pretty green-eyed blond, a little on the heavy side for my tastes but still very tasty, looking a couple of years younger than the guy—sort of barely ripe—in her tiny yellow two-piece.

The other girl's towel was empty.

Climbing the goat trail I did a quick scan of the beach. I couldn't find her anywhere. About ten feet from the top I turned and looked again. Nothing.

"I'm up here," she said.

I almost fell right off the trail. It would have been a bad fall.

It was very matter-of-fact, though, the way she said it. As though it were obvious I'd be looking for her. As though she simply knew. I turned and saw her standing there above me, and I think I must have flushed a little, because she smiled.

I climbed the trail to the top. I watched my footing, not because I really needed to, but because, as I say, it's my habit, and because it was sort of hard to look at her directly. Bathing suit or no, I don't think I'd ever seen anybody look so naked before.

Maybe it was the fact that she seemed so comfortable in her own skin, like a kid who doesn't know about clothes much.

But there was something consciously erotic about her too and a long haul from innocence. Just in the way she stood there, flicking a green-and-white bathtowel at the hawkweed, hipshot.

The breeze had died down long ago.

The sun put red and brown into the still dark hair.

I have seen the Caribbean since then. Toward the end of the day the sea sparkles with light as the sun goes down, and the color is that high transparent blue that will turn gray and then finally black by nightfall. Her eyes were like that, the color of last light.

They took me in all at once, gobbled me up.

I wondered how old she was.

I think I mumbled hi.

"It *was* me, wasn't it?" I listened for hints of mockery in her voice. There weren't any.

"It was you. How'd you know?"

She smiled and the lips remained full even then. She didn't answer, though.

She looked at me for a moment and I looked back and there was that nakedness again, that easy nudity. She flicked the towel. The head of a daisy shot off into the dust. She turned and walked a few steps back to a dark green Mercedes parked between Rafferty's old Dodge and a white Corvair.

"Drive me home?"

"Sure."

She climbed into the passenger side. I walked around and got behind the wheel. The keys were in the ignition. I started it up.

"Where to?"

"Seven Willoughby. You know where it is?"

"Sure. Summer place?"

"Uh-huh."

"You don't sound too happy."

"I'm not. They call me at school and tell me they've got this wonderful place lined up for the summer. I drive up and here it is. On the way up everything has been *shrinking*—trees, houses, shrubs. So I wonder if I'm not shrinking too. This town's a little dull."

"Tell me about it."

"You go to school?"

"No."

I pulled the car out into the road. I'd never felt the least bit guilty about not going to college. I still didn't, not exactly, but it was getting close to that.

"You do, though, right?"

I am fabulous at conversation.

"Pine Manor over in Chestnut Hill. My last year. Steven goes to Harvard, and Kimberley's with me only a year behind, and her major's French. Mine's Physical Anthropology. I'll do field work in another year if I want to bother."

"Do you?"

"So far. Sure. Why not. Don't you get bored?"

"Huh?"

"Don't you get bored around here?"

"Often."

"What do you do?"

"For a living?"

"I mean to kill the tedium."

"Oh, this and that. I see the beach a lot."

"I bet you do."

The road was narrow and twisting but I knew it blind by now, so it was easy to keep an eye on her. There was a small patch of sand on her shoulder. I wanted to brush it off, just for the excuse to touch her. She sat very low in the seat. She really was in terrific physical condition. Just one thin line where the flesh had to buckle at the stomach. She smelled lightly of dampness. Sweat and seawater.

"Your car?" I asked her. "It runs pretty good."

"No."

"You dad's?"

"No."

"Whose, then?"

She shrugged, telling me it didn't matter. "Is this your town? You've lived here all your life and all?"

"Me and my father both."

"You like it?"

"Not much."

"Then why stick around?"

"Inertia, I guess. Nothing ever came along to move me out."

"Would you like to have something come along and move you out?"

"Never thought about it. I don't know."

"So think about it. What if something did? Would you want that?"

"You want me to think about it right now?"

"You going anywhere?"

"No."

So I did. It was a hell of an odd question right off the bat like that but I gave it some thought. And while I was doing that I was wondering why she'd asked.

"I guess I might.Yeah."

"Good."

"Why good?"

"You're cute."

"So?"

"So I couldn't be bothered if you were stupid."

There wasn't much to say to that. The road wound by. I watched her staring out the window. The sun was going down. There were bright streaks of red in her hair. The line of neck to shoulder was very soft and graceful.

We were coming into town. Willoughby was just on the outskirts, the closest thing we could claim to a grouping of "better" houses.

"You'd better pull up here."

"You're not going home?"

She laughed. "Not in this. Pull up here."

I thought she meant the bathing suit, that her parents were strict about that. It was pretty skimpy. I pulled the car off to the shoulder and cut the engine. I reached for the keys.

"Leave them."

She opened the door and stepped out.

"I don't get it. What are you going to do about the car?"

She was already walking away. I slammed the door and caught up with her.

"I'm going to leave it here."

"With the keys in the ignition?"

"Sure."

Suddenly it dawned on me.

"I think you'd better tell me your name. So I know where to send them when they come for me."

She laughed again. "Casey Simpson White. Seven Willoughby Lane. And it will be my first offense. How about you?"

"Dan Thomas. I've been up against it before, I guess."

"What for?"

"They got me once when I was five. Me and another kid set fire to his backyard with a can of lighter fluid. That was one thing."

"There's more?"

"A little later, yeah. Nothing glamorous as auto theft, though. You wouldn't be interested."

I grabbed her arm. I could still feel the adrenaline churning. I couldn't help it. I'd never stolen a car before. It made me nervous. Her skin was soft and smooth. She didn't pull away.

"*Are you crazy*?"

She stopped and looked me straight in the eye.

"Buy me a drink and find out for yourself."

It was my turn to laugh then. "You're underage, though, right? You would have to be."

"Just."

"Please remember you never told me that. Come on."

Three

SO THAT WAS THE BUSINESS WITH THE CAR, and that was the first time she scared me.

The truth was I liked it.

Here was a girl, I thought, who didn't play by our rules—who hardly seemed to know them. And I guess I'd seen enough of rules in twenty years of Dead River.

It was rules that got you where you were and more rules

that kept you there, kids turning into premature adults, adults putting the hard day's work for wife and more kids and mortgaged house and car, and nobody ever got out from under. That was rule number one. You didn't get out. I'd seen it happen to my parents. The rule said, see, your foot is in the bear trap now and you're the one that put it there, so don't expect to come away alive; we didn't set it up for that. The problem was always money. The slightest twitch in the economy would sluice tidal waves through the whole community. We were always close to oblivion. The price of fish would change in Boston and half the town would be lined up at the bank, begging for money.

It might have made us tougher, but it didn't. All you saw were the stooped shoulders and the slow crawl toward bitterness and old age.

I'd moved out on my parents three years ago, when it became too hard to watch my father come up broke and empty after another season hauling in sardines in Passamaquoddy Bay and to watch my mother's house go slowly down around her. They were good people, and they were fools, and after a while all I could bring to them was anger.

At the time I didn't even know what I was so mad about, but I knew it wasn't working. So I found myself the job at the yard and then a little two-room apartment over Brody's Hardware on Main Street, and I'd stop by the house whenever I could stand it, which wasn't often.

Every now and then I'd wonder why I didn't get out entirely. The answer was the one I gave Casey. Inertia. A tired life breeds tired decisions, sometimes none at all. I was lazy. Demoralized. Always had been.

Then Casey.

And it was wonderful to see her thumb her nose at us; it was a pleasure. I'd always been too much a part of the town to really do it right. You needed to be an outsider for that, or at least you needed one to show you how. Someone with no worries about reputations, someone whose father didn't drink with the mayor and half the cops in town, someone with no stake.

Even if I hadn't wanted her, I might have gone along for the ride.

But I did want her. As I sat in the bar that day, she was just about all I wanted. Everything else looked kind of puny and small. It was only lust, but it had very big teeth.

What I'm trying to say here is that she got me started moving toward a lot of things, things I'd been avoiding for a long time. And I've never regretted that part of it for a minute. And I've never looked back.

Today, that part's still good.

Some of it, though.

Some of it was horrible.

And I'd better get into that right now, so I can set myself to thinking about it, getting it right. Otherwise the rest will make no sense to anybody, and I *know* there was a kind of sense to it, almost an inevitability, as though what happened was sure to happen given what we were together and what the town had become. It's a hard connection to make but I've got to make it. And maybe then I can just go on.

The Crouch place.

The subject came up early between us, and then I guess, just hung there unnoticed on the borders of her memory like a cobweb in an attic full of old toys.

Wish to god I'd seen the spider.

We were sitting at the soda fountain at Harmon's General Store because Steven had been bothering us for a chocolate egg cream all day long, and we finally got tired of his gritting his teeth and hissing at us as though he had to go to the bathroom something awful and nobody would let him, so we went to Harmon's and he explained the drink to Mrs. Harmon. A hefty squirt of chocolate syrup, a little milk, and lots of seltzer. Mrs. Harmon kept shaking her head. "No egg?"

As usual the conversation got around to bitching about how nothing ever happened here and how there was nothing to do, so

I happened to mention the Crouch place and what happened when we were kids.

You may have read about the end of it if you get the Boston papers. I know the *Globe* carried a story on it, because Rafferty and I both kept our copies until they got yellow and dog-eared. Dead River gets so little scandal. So we read the story over and over. How the police and the ASPCA broke in, now that Ben and Mary were gone. Testimony from Mr. Harmon and Chief Peters. For a while you'd get these wacky types driving up especially, just to see the place, though there wasn't much to see.

All they did see was an old, ramshackle two-story house on Winslow Homer Avenue—a tiny dirt road on the outskirts of town that ran all the way back to the sea. It sat on a three-acre plot of land, the front yard and the forest beyond long since combined and climbing the broken stairs to the gray, weathered front door. Vines and creepers everywhere. Out back, a narrow slip of land sloped to the edge of a cliff, below which was the ocean.

Never once did I see them as a boy. Ben and Mary Crouch had disappeared into the dank interior of that house long before my time. I heard rumors, though. We all did. Talk among our parents that led us to think there was something "not right" about Ben and Mary. Beyond that good parents wouldn't go, not with the kids around. But it was enough. Because later there were more rumors, which we ourselves created.

How they ate children and lived inside huge cocoons spun from the flesh of babies. How they were really living corpses, vampires, witches, zombies.

The usual thing.

Once, when I was ten, three of us got up the nerve to run around to the back of the house and peer into their garbage.

They lived completely out of cans.

There was not a piece of paper wrap or a frozen-food box or a shred of lettuce anywhere. Just cans. Canned fruit, canned peas, carrots, onions. Canned meats and tuna from S. S. Pierce. And every can had been wiped or washed so that it was spotless.

I can't tell you why that odd bit of cleanliness upset us so. But it did.

There was dog food—also canned—and lots of it. We counted five separate bagfuls.

Everybody knew they kept dogs, though how many dogs was a matter of conjecture. But it wasn't just two or three. The place had an unmistakably doggy smell to it. The stink of unwashed fur and dog shit. You could smell it yards away. But there were no neighbors around to complain. Not for miles. Just a forest of scrub pine and brambles out of which the house seemed to rise as though out of a tangled green cloud, moving densely back to the sea.

We looked into the garbage and peeked through the basement window. It was much too dark to see in there. But Jimmy Beard swore he saw something sway and move in the darkness.

We did not argue. We ran. As though the stories we'd made up were true. As though hell itself could come pouring out of there.

And I can feel my hackles rise as I write this, remembering how it felt that day.

Because maybe, in a way, we were right.

Here's what made the papers:

I was thirteen I think when the police came and opened up the place.

It was a delivery boy from Harmon's who had called them after a month went by with all the cans piling up unopened, untouched, on the porch and no slip in the mailbox with his payment.

They opened the front door with a crowbar, two cops and the delivery boy, and one of the cops came very close to losing his hand. Because behind the door were twenty-three dogs. And all of them were starving.

They sealed the house up again and called in troops. The next day half the town was out there, me and Rafferty included. It was quite a show. Six policemen and Jack Gardener, the sad old drunk who was our dog warden, and six or seven guys in white lab jackets from the ASPCA in Machias dumping whole sackfuls of dog food into the house through a punched-in hole in the front kitchen window, then settling back, waiting, while the snapping sounds and the growling and howling and eating sounds wore away at everybody's nerves.

Then when it was quiet again they moved in with nets and stun-pistols. And I had my first look inside the place.

I couldn't see how they'd lived there. Once the house had been somebody's pride. I remember being told it was a hundred years old or more. There were hand-hewn beams in the ceiling, and the wood on the doors and moldings were it wasn't stained and smeared with god knows what was still good high-quality cedar and oak. But the rest was incredible. Filthy. Foul. Floors caked with dog shit, reeking of urine. Old newspapers stacked everywhere, almost reaching the ceiling in some places, damp and yellow. A couch and an overstuffed chair torn to shreds, pieces of them scattered everywhere. The refrigerator door hung open, empty. Cabinets and doors were chewed and clawed to splinters.

A few of us kids stood at the front door, making twisted faces at the stink. We watched them as they brought out the dogs one by one and locked them into the ASPCA van. Many had to be carried out, they were so weak. And all of them were pretty docile after the feeding. I wondered if they'd dropped some drugs in there too. I remember a lot of them looked sort of bewildered, dazed. They were pathetically thin.

I stopped looking when they found the bodies.

There were four of them. One was just a puppy. One was a Doberman. The other two had been medium-sized mutts.

Obviously the other dogs had eaten them.

My father arrived.

He was pretty angry. He pulled me into the car and then just sat there, snorting, shaking his head, his face getting redder and redder. I knew he wanted to hit me, and I knew how hard it was for him not to.

I guessed I'd disappointed him again.

So I told them all this over two rounds of egg creams. I had them wide-eyed.

"Ben and Mary they never found, by the way."

"*Never*?" Steven had this habit of pointing his index finger at you when he asked a question as though he were accusing you of lying. He would also dip his head a little and look at you up from under those dark eyebrows. I think he was practicing for the law. It was very astute-looking.

"Never. We got some clues, though, about a week later. At least you could figure *why* they'd disappeared. All of a sudden the big word around town was that the bank had evicted them the month before for nonpayment of their mortgage. So it looked like they just ignored the notices for a while, and then, when Ben Murphy went out there to tell them face-to-face that they'd have to leave, they just listened and nodded and then when he was gone, they just cleared out."

"Awful thing to do to all those dogs, though." Kimberley slurped the bottom of her glass through the long striped straw. "So *cruel*. How could you care for all those animals and then be so rotten to them?"

"People do it all the time," said Steven.

Casey leaned toward me. "Did they look for them? Ben and whatsername, Mary, I mean?"

"Sure they did. I don't know how hard, though. The eviction business seemed to explain things well enough, so I don't know how hard anybody worried about it, really.

"About the dogs, though. See, there was a lot of talk after that. My mom and dad, for one thing, were a lot more free about discussing it in front of me. And I remember being shocked at the time to hear a friend of my mother's say that Ben and Mary were brother and sister, and only in their thirties. We'd always pictured them as withered ancients, you know—and married. The evil old man and his witchy wife. Not so.

"But here's the important part. They'd been raised, both of

them, in the bughouse. Literally. At Augusta Mental. Till they were in their teens. The schizo son and daughter of a crazy Boston combat-zone stripper, alky too I guess. So you have to wonder what kind of shape they were in to worry about a pack of dogs, you know?"

"Geez."

"You sure about that?" There was that index finger again and two inches of arched eyebrow.

"Sure as I can be. At least that was the current lie going around at the time."

"Geez."

"Good story," said Casey.

And it was. Good enough, certainly, to wile away an hour over sodas at Harmon's. But it still left us with nothing to do. Workmen had stripped the Crouch place and refinished it, and for a couple of years a retired doctor and his wife had lived there, civilized it presumably, tamed it. So that now, even though the old man was no longer there and the house lay empty, it was just another house in the woods. Nothing you'd want to visit.

It had amused us, though, back then when we were kids. For the next few years Dead River had its very own haunted house. Somewhere to go to scare yourself on Halloween. That was before the doctor came in.

Teenage folklore being what it is, our stories about Ben and Mary just got wilder.

They were really dead, for one thing. Their ghosts had frightened workmen cleaning up the basement. They could be heard calling dogs on foggy, rainy nights. Some of these yarns I started myself, before I outgrew them.

My favorite turned on the disappearance itself.

According to this one the eviction never happened. The truth was that the dogs had turned on Ben and Mary and eaten them. Every scrap. Bones and all. I liked that story. I think that Rafferty made it up. I kept remembering all those lost, dazed eyes.

I thought the dogs deserved their revenge.

Four

I THINK I TOLD THEM ABOUT BEN AND MARY two or three days after we met, no more. By then Casey and I were thinking about becoming lovers.

That first afternoon in the bar I had all I could do to keep the small talk running and keep my hands off her. I'm not stupid. There are girls you push and girls you don't. And there are some who only want you if they can see no particular need in you, who want to know you're calm enough and tough enough to live with or without them. Girls like Casey want calm and confidence. You did not have to be a genius to see that rushing her would mean a long walk home alone.

So I sat on my hands and tried to keep it nice and easy, willing but not eager.

I walked home alone anyway.

I was coming back from the diner on the corner that same night when I saw them drive by in the white Chevy. All three of them waved at me, laughing. But the car didn't stop.

I figured that was that.

The conversation in the bar had been innocuous, probably too innocuous, and now I was the local horse's ass.

Not so.

They stopped by the lumberyard at lunchtime the next day.

I was around back, using the forklift on a stack of four-by-fours. Casey came out through the back of the store and when I pulled around for another set of chocks, I damn near took her head off with the lift blades. If the manager had seen her there that close to me I'd have lost the job then and there. I turned the thing off and climbed off it.

"They fire you for disemboweling a customer."

"What customer? I'm your cousin from New Paltz. Your aunt—my mother—is over at the house and probably she's dying.

Her last wish is to see her sister and her favorite nephew. You've got the day off. It's all fixed. I didn't even have to ask for it."

"Huh?"

"He said I could tell you just to go home for the day."

"You assume a lot, you know that?"

"Sure I do. You mad at me?"

The way she asked me, it was a serious question, nothing coy about it. If I thought she'd gone too far, then she wanted to know. I liked that. Even though I had the feeling that my answer was not going to make or break her afternoon either way.

"I'm not mad. It's too hot for this stuff anyway. Let's go."

We walked through the store and I said thanks to Mr. McGregor, and I was glad he was with a customer just then, because I could see Kim and Steven right out front sitting in the Chevy, waiting for us with the top down. A suspicious-looking bunch of New Paltz cousins.

"Dan Thomas, Steven Lynch and Kimberley Palmer."

"Kimberley."

She wiped her hand on her shorts, a nervous, bird-like movement. Then she held it out to me and I took it. It was tiny and delicate, and very smooth and dry.

Steven smiled at me and nodded and gave me a slightly too-firm handshake. We got into the car. It was a tight squeeze. I glanced back over my shoulder at Mr. McGregor.

"Could we get out of here, please? Fast?"

"Sure thing."

He floored it. I couldn't help wincing. I pictured Mr. McGregor rushing to the window, watching four kids in an antique convertible fishtailing out of his parking lot. Already I was wondering what sort of approach to use with him tomorrow. There would be feathers on my boss that needed smoothing.

You had to yell over the howl of wind.

"Where to?" I asked them.

Casey's breath was warm in my ear. "The beach. But first we want to stop at Shop 'N' Save. Pick up a few things."

"Fine."

Steven switched the radio on and turned up the volume, and after that there was no possibility of talking at all. His long slim fingers beat time against the steering wheel. I could smell Casey's perfume in sudden gusts, a clean smell, with nothing sweet or musky about it. Kim looked back at us from the front seat and smiled. The smile was crooked, but the teeth were white and dazzling.

We pulled into the Shop 'N' Save lot, and all of us piled out. Casey reached under the driver's seat and pulled out a green book bag with a long strap and slung it over her shoulder.

"Get us a couple six-packs, will you, Dan? Steve, see if you can find some decent crackers this time, okay?"

Steven held the door for us, smiling, then flinched at the blast of cold air. I was the only one dressed for the air-conditioning. They always overdo it in these chain stores. You could keep corpses back there and they'd never decompose. Both girls were wearing shorts and halters, and Steve had on what I came to know as his usual gaudy Hawaiian-type short-sleeve shirt. With the thin white linen slacks he looked prosperous and trendy and very cold.

I went for the beer.

I had to do some digging for the Heineken dark, so by the time I had that and the two six-packs of Bud to the checkout stand, Steve was already there ahead of me, paying for two boxes of crackers. "See you outside," he said, shivering.

I paid for the beer, and as the girl was packing it up for me I saw Kim step into line in back of the woman behind me. She had a large loaf of french bread under her arm and some butter and was smiling at me in a strange, uncomfortable kind of way. Then I saw her eyes move along, following something behind me. I turned around.

And there was Casey, walking out the front door easy as you please. From the look of the green book bag, she'd stuffed it with apples and watermelon.

I lifted my own bag and walked outside. Casey had already gotten in the back, and Steven was starting her up. I handed her my bag and she looked at me. The pale blue eyes were sly and humorous.

"You don't approve."

"I don't disapprove, either."

"We only steal from chain stores."

"And I suppose they can afford it."

"And we only steal delicacies. Look."

She dumped the book bag onto the seat. There were two big jars of Icelandic caviar. Smoked sausages. Pâtés, liver and fois gras. Cheeses. Oysters. Squid.

"We've got lunch, anyway."

"We sure do. It doesn't bother you?"

"Why should it bother me?"

"It's your town."

"But not my chain store."

She seemed to relax a bit. I wondered if I'd just passed some sort of test with her. I wondered how many more to expect, and how many more I'd want to deal with. She stared at me a long moment more than was comfortable.

Then Kim came out to the car, giggling. She glanced at the backseat.

"Good haul?"

"The best. Hop in."

There was something in the tone of it. "*Hop in.*" The words were addressed to Kimberley but I thought they were meant for me. I guessed I was along for the ride. Something did a little two-step across my spine.

"To the beach!"

"Ever go skinny-dipping out this way?"

Steve was doing an unhealthy seventy along the narrow, winding road, but he still thought he had enough control to be able to shout at me over his shoulder. He didn't. I leaned in close so he wouldn't have to do it again.

"Not here. Over at Echo Beach maybe. There's a couple places at Bar Harbor."

"Why not here?

"Police. They frown on it."

"Fuck that."

He turned completely around to face me again, half-smiling, half-scowling. His wicked look.

Odd guy, I thought. I wondered what his connection was to the women. There was the obvious urge to impress them. The loud colors. The fast driving. He had a peculiar way of glancing at Casey no matter who he was speaking to. It wasn't just a matter of including her. It seemed to have something to do with approval. He was a good-looking guy, with dark, even features, sort of Latin and WASP combined. But there was something insecure about him. I had the feeling that in a way he was just as much a stranger to all this as I was.

You could make an educated guess that he was a bit hung up on Casey. That would account for the sidelong glances. But then what was he doing paired up to Kimberley? Certainly she thought they were an item, even if he didn't. Her blond downy arm draped itself gracefully over his shoulders as he drove. Every now and then her hand would move up to play with the hair along the back of his neck or behind his ears. When he spoke she listened very attentively. Her gaze was proprietary. He didn't return it very much, and when he did, it was without heat.

I wondered how deep the bravado ran. I decided to call him on the nudity bit. See how he reacted. I knew a beach where the stones were pretty smooth and the waves rolled in easily somewhat to the north of here. You could do a bit of swimming. It was secluded enough. Nobody bothered with it much except the shell hunters.

"Take your next right," I told him.

To be honest, I wasn't opposed to seeing how the girls reacted, either.

We turned down an old dirt road and drove half a mile

through the Guiles farmland, then slowed down as the road turned rougher through the dark pine forest than Van and I used to play in as kids.

Van was my older brother. He died in 'Nam when I was thirteen. It was two days after my birthday, November 12.

My father and Mr. Guiles were old friends. But we never came out here again after Van died. Maybe that was because his own son, Billy, had the bad grace to survive intact while Van went down in a burning helicopter over Khe Sanh. Maybe it was just too many memories. But we stayed away.

I remembered it, though. It hadn't changed much. Forest roads take a long time to change. A little rockier, maybe, but just the same. It gave me a pleasant feeling, like coming home.

Steven cursed the road so hard you'd have thought it was his car and not Casey's. But it opened up soon and got smoother, and then there was that familiar little stretch of meadow and the cabin we used to call the Picnic Basket. Steve pulled over and parked, and we took the food from the car. Casey was first to discover the view. I walked over to her.

"Pretty good, isn't it."

"Wonderful."

We stood thirty feet above a shallow bay with all the Atlantic back-dropped behind it. Directly below was a rocky beach. There were boulders and crumbled slate.

When the seas were rough the water rose to maybe fifteen feet from where we were standing. All the contours would seem to change overnight. If you came here as infrequently as I did, it was never the same place twice.

I led them down a path to the sea. We found a spot beside a thick column of slate ten feet from the rock face and deposited our stolen merchandise and our towels. I climbed to the top of the column.

The gulls had been here, as I'd thought they would. They smashed the shells of crabs and clams and oysters against the rock to get at the softer stuff inside. It was littered with tiny corpses.

I saw Casey watching me and waved her up. She was a good climber.

"See this? Seagulls' restaurant."

She stooped to examine the dry empty shell of a blue-claw crab.

"They fly over here and drop them. Their aim is very good. Usually, that does it. If not, it will crack them a little. So they find the cracks and do the rest with their beaks. They'd probably be here now if it weren't for us. See?"

We watched them wheel through the blue-gray sky a quarter of a mile away.

"You know about things like that?"

"About the sea? Some."

"What else do you know about? Tell me."

I shrugged.

"Lumber. Wood. Henry Miller. Dostoevsky. I can make a fire with a couple of sticks if I really have to. I build a pretty comfortable campsite. I know about Dead River, what there is of it. I cook a pretty decent fried egg. Not much, actually.

"What about me?"

"What about you?"

"What do you know about me?"

"I can guess some things."

"Yes, but what are you sure of?"

"Nothing."

"Liar."

She stood up and moved her hand around behind her back and I saw the halter shudder free. She slipped it off and tossed it away. It drifted down the rock and settled below.

Her breasts were small, firm, with a high lift to them. Beautiful. She stared at me. There was hard challenge in the blue eyes. Challenge but no mockery. She stooped a little and drew down the white shorts over her hips. She wore nothing underneath. The pubic hair was sparse and delicate, a light golden brown. She watched me through all this and then smiled.

"Now you know more."

"Now I do."

She turned away and moved easily down the rock, agile as a cat.

She walked toward Steve and Kimberley. I watched her. There was a stupid grin on my face and very little immediate possibility of making it go away. I watched the easy grace of her. There was nothing to do but stand there until the muscles of my face worked again.

The others got out of their clothes.

Kimberley had larger breasts than I'd have expected. They were heavy-nippled, slung low and wide apart but very pretty, very lush. She had a prominent mound of red-gold public hair. A little more in hip and thigh than I'd have asked for in the best of all possible worlds, but very much a green-eyed eyeful.

Steven was hung like a ranch animal.

And he wasn't shy at all.

I have cheap thoughts sometimes. They just come to me, unbidden. I had one now. I thought I was beginning to understand why Kim kept looking at him so fondly.

I couldn't keep my eyes off Casey.

She waded into the sea and I watched the frigid water tighten her skin again. I thought I'd never see anything so beautiful. She looked up at me, and I felt a clear silent summons. The grin was gone by then, so I climbed down off the rock. Compared to her I felt clumsy. A little muscle but no style.

"Come on in."

"You're kidding."

"Oh, come *on*. It's no big deal."

"Neither is pneumonia."

She swirled the water gently around her calves.

"Now look. Steven doesn't swim and Kim's chicken. Are you going to make me do this all by myself?"

"I'll get my jeans wet."

"So take them off."

"My shirt, then."

"That too." She laughed.

What the hell, I thought. It was an easy way to get naked in front of them. I needed an excuse.

I let the clothes lie where I dropped them. I saw her watching me and felt two sets of eyes from behind. Hope it's up to snuff, I thought. But I've never been much for display. So as soon as I moved out of my shorts I ran for the water. She dove in ahead of me. The last thing I saw was a slim pair of legs sliding into the water, toes pointed. A clean, perfect dive.

Mine was not so perfect. As soon as I hit the water I went rigid with the sheer numbing shock of it. It was like diving into a vat of scotch on the rocks. Colder.

I exploded to the surface with a shout. Pure agony. Then immediately I felt her arm around my waist, so I shook the water out of my eyes and grabbed for her, laughed and heard her laughing and pulled her to me hard while she did the same to me. And suddenly there was body heat between us, enough to make the water seem fifteen degrees warmer.

I felt her hand slide over my buttocks and I pulled her closer still, and felt myself rising through the tiny space of freezing water so that just a moment later I was nestled between her legs. Her laugh was more private this time, just for the two of us. She scissored her legs together, trapping me in there, in a small hot nexus between them. I must have groaned.

"Not yet," she said softly. "Not yet but very soon."

And that was the first time I kissed her, there in the deathly freezing sea.

The taste of her was salty. Her mouth was rich and soft, all tongue and teeth and roaring heat.

When we came out of the water Kim was smiling at us. The classic cat-and-the-canary grin. Though it was caviar on her fingertips and not bird meat. She looked at us and spread her arms so that the breasts jiggled slightly and said, "Love!" Just that.

Steven pointed his finger at me.

"You having fun, buddy?"
"I am, yes."
We all laughed.
It wasn't love exactly. But it wasn't disinterest, either.

Five

MY PHONY AUNT TOOK A LONG TIME DYING.

We went to the beach almost every day. It was always the same place. We always stole our lunches. In one way or another, there was always the nude flirting.

Despite my resolve to be patient, my frustration level ran high. I began to wonder if Casey wasn't just another cold-assed tease. But there was something about her that was different from the others I'd met, a kind of questioning, a searching, a steady appraisal of me that seemed to carry a more serious intent than anything I was used to.

So I stuck around.

On the way back home one day I took them down the coast road toward Lubec. You could see the old house way off to the left, slouched against the cliffs in the dim half-light of dusk. Casey was driving and Steven sat in the back with me.

"That's the house," I told him. "The one I talked about."

"The Crouch place?"

"Yeah."

He turned around to have a look. By then we'd almost passed it. I was watching Casey's hair tossing in the wind. There is something about a handsome woman in a sports car that is one of the best things summer has to offer.

He turned back around and saw me watching her. I caught his expression: a slight frown. He'd been quiet with me lately. I knew there was jealousy there. But at the same time I felt a kind of tacit acceptance of me that hadn't been present at first, a knowledge that I was there for the duration. He was verging on the genuine. The gaudy Hawaiian shirt seemed slightly out of place now.

"I thought you said nobody lived there."

"Nobody does."

He shrugged. "I saw a light."

I turned around. The house was too far behind us now. All I saw was darkness.

"Where?"

"Upstairs. The second floor, I guess."

"That's impossible."

He shrugged again.

"I saw a light," he said.

I was drinking beers with Rafferty in the Caribou after work the following day. So I asked him. Rafferty collects a lot of scuttlebutt at the station.

"Is anybody in the Crouch place now?"

"You kidding?"

"No."

"Not that I heard of."

"That's what I thought."

"Why? You want to rent or something?"

His grin was slightly feral. Rafferty remembered the Crouch place as well as I did.

"We drove by last night. Steven said he thought he saw a light."

"Where?"

"In a second-floor window."

"He didn't see shit."

It came out pretty hostile. There was some resentment, I thought, of my relationship with these people. Maybe he was a little jealous. He'd seen Casey. And maybe he was already thinking what I was not—not yet—that they represented a way out of Dead River. They'd met Rafferty but had shown no interest. I hadn't pushed the matter. There was me and Casey and Steven and Kim. Two boys, two girls. Rafferty was not included.

"If anybody was out there, I'd know. They'd have to come by for gas now and then. Your friend was mistaken."

I knew that last bit was meant to soften it slightly.

"I guess he was, George."

We sipped our drinks. Rafferty stared straight ahead at the old Pabst clock over the bar. Then I saw a grin starting.

"Of course, I wouldn't know about kids playing out there."

I smiled back at him. "Now, what kid in his right mind would want to do that?"

"Wouldn't know."

It had been me and Rafferty once. We'd wanted to. And were much too spooked to try. We'd managed to get as far as the garbage cans and a peek through the cellar window before Jimmy Beard cried wolf on us and ran us off. Maybe kids were bolder now. The memory of it reunited us once again.

"You'd have to be completely crazy," he said.

"Completely."

He pulled on his beer, emptied it.

"God knows."

Six

IT HAD BEEN A MISERABLE DAY AT WORK. Too much heat. It frayed the customers' nerves and it frayed mine. I kept thinking of the beach, of Casey's belly tanning in the sun. It made me restless but it got me by.

I went home and showered and shaved, drank a cup of coffee and wolfed down a hamburger to go from The Sugar Bowl, a local greasy spoon. I dressed and went downstairs. The old black pickup, all body rust and squeaky hinges, stood waiting for me across the street. I drove to her place and parked it.

It was a very big house for three people to live in. I wondered if her mother had help with it. Help would be easy to find and cheap to hold in Dead River.

I climbed the steps to the freshly painted white front porch and rang the bell. There were lights on in the living room. I heard a deep sigh, then the sound of slow steps crossing the room.

Her father opened the door.

He was a big man, broad across the shoulders and still trim at somewhere around fifty, with thinning gray-brown hair, black-frame glasses and an inch or two of height on me—six-two or six-three. He looked tired. His color wasn't good. He blinked at me through the half-open door and I could see where Casey's eyes had come from, though his own were maybe one-quarter shade darker.

"Yes?"

I put out my hand.

"Dan Thomas, Mr. White. Casey's expecting me."

He looked sort of muddled and shook my hand distractedly. I wondered if the bad color came from drinking.

"Oh. Yes. Come in."

He moved aside and opened the door wider. I walked in. Inside the house was very handsome. A lot better than the usual summer rental. Most of the furnishings were old, antiques, not exactly top quality but in good condition. The wood looked freshly polished. And there was an old rolltop desk off to one corner that was a beauty.

He called up the stairs to her. The answer sounded rushed and far away.

"Coming!"

Neither of us sat. Nor were we able to think of much to say. I guessed he'd been reading the paper when I rang, because he was clutching it now, rolled up tight, in one big meaty fist. Sick or not, I wouldn't have wanted him mad at me.

Casey had said he was a banker, but it was hard to picture him hunched over a desk toting up a row of figures. Except for the sallow color you'd have pegged him for outdoor work. I wondered how he'd gotten those shoulders. Then I looked around the room a bit and saw the big framed photo on the wall over the desk, and that told me.

He saw me looking and smiled.

"Wrestling team. Yale, 1938. That's me, last one on the left. Had a pretty good record that year. Twelve wins, two losses."

"Not bad."

He sat down, sighing, in the big overstuffed chair beside the fireplace. There was no enthusiasm in his smooth baritone. It was flat, dead. Like the eyes were dead. They were Casey's eyes but there was nothing in them, no animation, not even the strange fathomlessness I found so attractive in hers. His eyes could have been colored glass. I wondered if he was sick, or even dying.

There was the inevitable small talk. What do you do for a living.

"I sell lumber."

He nodded meaninglessly. There was a silence. He was staring at something in front of him. I tried to follow his gaze but his question called me back.

"Can you make a living at that?"

"Barely. But there aren't too many options here. Boats make me seasick."

"Me too." He laughed. He wasn't amused, though. The laugh was meaningless too.

"Nice place you've got here."

I told you I was fabulous at conversation.

More nodding.

I was making all the impact of a spot on the rug. Luckily he didn't seem to care. I had the feeling that as far as he was concerned, I was barely there.

We heard footsteps on the stairs. He glanced up at me sharply and for once his eyes seemed to focus. Ah, a human being standing there.

"Take care of my daughter, Mr. Thomas."

"Yes, sir."

The footsteps descended. I saw him staring away from me again, and this time I followed the sight lines across the room to a small table cluttered with vase, flowers, ashtray, and a pair of gilt-frame photographs. One was a few-years-old photo of Casey. A high school graduation photo, probably. The other was a studio portrait of a young brown-eyed boy, maybe six or seven years old, smiling in that shy funny way kids have of smiling without showing you their teeth.

Casey had never mentioned a brother.

I looked at Mr. White. He was staring intently at the photographs. The high-pale forehead was studded with creases. The flesh gleamed. I wondered if it was Casey he was staring at or the boy.

"Ready?"

She swung down the stairs and the T-shirt looked painted on. By a very steady hand. She stood there slightly out of breath, smiling, smelling very clean and freshly showered.

"Let's go," I said.

She moved to her father and pecked him on the cheek.

"Bye, Daddy."

He managed to raise a weak smile. I could not see much in the way of affection between them.

"You'll be late?"

"Don't know. Maybe. Say good night to mother for me."

"Yes."

He stood up absentmindedly but with some effort. It was learned behavior but its hold on him was stronger than the discomfort it caused him. Or that's how it looked to me. When a lady leaves the room, you stand. Even if it's your daughter. It was years of habit talking. But it wasn't making life any easier for him

Like everything else I'd seen him do, its net effect was zero. Except to make you wonder where all that lethargy came from. Here was a man, I thought, inhabiting a great big void.

"Good night...young man," he said

He'd forgotten my name.

"Good night, sir."

We walked outside into the warm summer night. I was glad to be out of there.

She looked at the pickup across the street.

"You really want to take that thing?"

"I don't care."

"Let's take the Chevy, then. Kim and Steve would never forgive me."

She turned and headed for the driveway. I grabbed her arm.

"Suppose we make a deal?"

"What's that."

"We take the Chevy. But tonight we skip Kim and Steve."

She laughed. "They're expecting us."

"Call in sick. Say you've got your period."

"I can't do that."

"Sure you can."

"Suppose they see us driving around town or something?"

I shrugged. "You got better again."

We climbed into the car. I watched her mull it over for a minute. She was smiling and I had the feeling I was winning this one. She started up the car. I leaned over and took her chin in my hand, turned her toward me and kissed her. At first I kissed smiling lips and teeth. Then there was heat and a brittle hunger.

She pulled away.

"You convinced me."

We drove to the phone booth in front of Harmon's. She got out, and I watched her under neon light. Dialing the number, talking. I guess she got a little argument. Then she turned toward me and made a circle with her thumb and forefinger. A moment later she smiled and hung up. She climbed back into the car and slammed the door.

"I have my period. Kim will tell Steven. He's not going to like it much. But."

"But."

I kissed her.

"What is it with Steven, anyway?"

"You mean with Steven and me."

I nodded. She laughed at me.

"We were kids together. Next-door neighbors. When we were real little, we even talked about getting married some day. You know how kids do. Then we grew up. At least some of us did."

"He's going to Harvard."

"There are plenty of kids at Harvard, dear."

"So where does Kim come into it?"

"Oh, some seven or eight years later. I met her in junior high. I introduced them. His parents and mine and Kim's all became friends eventually anyway, so they'd have met sooner or later. All the same, I take complete credit for putting that together. And I'll tell you, back in high school it was a very heavy thing. They were both sort of...precocious, I guess you'd say. Kim developed quite a reputation. Deservedly, of course."

"And they've been together all this time?"

"We have. *We've* stayed together. Sometimes I feel like we're linked at the hip, the three of us. We've had some rough spots, but they pass. If you want me, you take Kim. And if you want Kim, you take me. Steve wants both of us, so its' easy. It's a weird relationship. We've never been lovers, never will be. But he's still sort of possessive of me, you know? And without me, I'm not sure he and Kim would still be together. Like I say, I think he wants us both—both together. And he can only get me through Kim.

"I don't know how it works, actually. But I think I'm the glue in all this, somehow. And to answer your next question, yes, sometimes it is a big pain in the ass. But not usually."

I decided to throw her a curve ball, as long as she was in the mood to put up with my curiosity. I made it very casual-sounding.

"So where does your brother fit in?"

"My *brother*?"

Whatever it was, it came up fast and mean. I felt I knew

how the rat feels when the trap snaps shut—it was such a *tiny* piece of cheese in the first place. There was suddenly something dangerous scuttling around in the car with us.

"Who the hell mentioned my brother? Daddy?"

"I just saw his picture, that's all. In the living room. So I wondered."

She stared at me a moment, and I knew how cold those eyes could be. She twisted the key in the ignition and the car sprang obediently to life. She pulled away. The tires screeched at us.

"*Let's just forget about my fucking brother*," she said.

I made a mental note to damn well try.

There was a local band at the Caribou that night. It was pretty bad. Two guitarists, a fat lazy drummer, and a girl lead singer I vaguely remembered from high school. She was small and blond and squeaky, with no breasts at all and the stage presence of a plate of peach preserves. Their repertoire was entirely cribbed from Loretta Lynn and Ernest Tubb records. You dreamed wistfully of bad Top 40. We drank our beers and when the boys in front stood up and applauded "Waltz Across Texas" we got the hell out of there.

She wanted to drive around some.

I talked and she listened. There was the urge to tell her everything, to give her the complete thumbnail Dan Thomas. But I held back here and there, wanting to keep it light. I avoided mention of my own brother. I didn't want her to think I was leading back to hers. What I wanted was just to amuse her, but there wasn't much I could think of that was very amusing. And as I talked I realized just how depressing Dead River was, compared to what she was used to in Boston. Compared to anything. But it was all I had.

So I told her about Rafferty and the night he and the Borkstrom twins got drunk and crapped in old man Lymon's water tower. I told her about the drag races through Becker's Flats. I told her about the old black dog we used to have who could whistle through his teeth. And I wondered what in the world she was making of all this, and of me.

She wanted to know why I'd been caught setting fire to somebody's back lawn. I told her we were napalming plastic soldiers.

But it was uncomfortably close to the other thing.

So I drew her off of that.

It started to rain.

Just a light warm drizzle with a heavy fog rolling in.

We'd left the top down on the Chevy, so we pulled over across the street from the Colony Theater, got out and hauled it out of the well and snapped the snaps down. Across the street the movie was *Children Shouldn't Play with Dead Things*, one of those low-budget horror pictures. But I guess there wasn't much business. Candy Bailey sat in the booth reading a paperback mystery. The streets were quiet.

Casey walked over to me. I had my hand on the door handle on the driver's side, ready to let her back inside. She put her fingers down lightly on my forearm.

"Wait. Come here."

Necking in the streets.

It felt pretty awkward at first. It was my town after all and there was Candy Bailey in the lighted booth a few yards away. The feeling didn't last, though. Only a few seconds before her mouth convinced me that it was a very good thing to do. After the first long kiss we parted and I saw how the tiny droplets of rain glistened in her hair under the theater lights from across the street. I saw the look on her face. The unexpected hunger there.

We kissed again. Long and wanting and hard this time, an animal shifting of the muscles along her back.

A man walked by behind us, walking a big mongrel dog, just a shadow in front of the closed-up shell of a drugstore that had failed three years ago. I was only just aware of him.

Her body fit with mine like none I'd ever held before, every curve and hollow melting into a perfect whole. Her tongue tasted sweet. It flayed the inside of my mouth until the only thing in the world I wanted to do was climb back into that car and finish it before I exploded at her. Drive to my place. Feel her naked on the cool fresh sheets, damp with sweat.

Her hand moved mine beneath the T-shirt to her naked breast and belly. They felt hot to the touch. There was a fragrant woman-smell rising off her flesh. She moaned softly against my mouth and moved us back against the Chevy.

"Lift me up."

"You'll ruin the skirt."

It was soft white linen.

"I don't care."

I moved my hands to her thighs and hitched her up onto the low front hood of the car. She wrapped her arms around me and kissed me again.

The kiss was furious, amazing, touched with something crazy running between us like a thin white-hot wire. When it was over we pulled back and gasped for breath, chests heaving, hearts pounding. Her eyes glittered as she looked at me.

The rain had begun to come down a little harder.

My face was so flushed I felt we must have been steaming there, the two of us, boiling mists off the street. I'd never thought it possible to want a woman this bad. I could feel the ache for her in every bone in my body, through every inch of skin. And in a way just wanting her that much was enough, fulfillment of a kind. Had a car come along just then and plowed us down I'd have died in the rainslick streets a happy man. Just to have had the moment. That pleasure, that desire.

So I wasn't prepared for the rest.

I saw her eyes glance away from me, over my shoulder to the theater. The eyes were wide, her face wet and gleaming with rain. Her voice was a soft passionate whisper.

"She's watching. She *sees* us."

"We can go to my place."

"No."

"Please, Casey."

"*No*."

She pulled me close. She took my hand again and moved it slowly under her skirt. I felt the coolness of her thigh turn slowly to a sleek humid warmth as she moved it upward. Then there was only the soft thin tuft of pubic hair under my hand and the naked depth of her.

"*Here.*" Her lips stung my cheek. "*Right here and now or not at all.*"

Then suddenly she was all teeth and shifting flesh that turned and stroked and grappled with me.

And suddenly the rain began in earnest.

A flash of light and rain and wind that rattled the storefront behind me, followed by a distant thunder.

And there on the rain-drenched glistening streets of my hometown I saw the strange wild pleasure in her face as she looked behind me and saw a girl I'd known since childhood watch me plunge into her like a prisoner, like a starving man, between naked thighs clamped hard around my hips and waist, and heard her laugh with a terrible, awesome kind of greed as I threw up her yellow T-shirt and felt the breasts soften and flush beneath my hands. And then the moisture inside her flowed and flowed until I poured myself into her and stood still, trembling, finished.

They say that on a fighter the legs go first.

I dropped slowly to the black street, water running over my knees. Not caring.

I looked up and saw her smile and slide down off the car, breathing through her open mouth. She gave me her hand.

The wind whistled through the tree in front of Harmon's, broken long ago by lightning.

"We can go now," she said.

Seven

That night we slept together on my bed. In the morning she was gone when I woke. There was no note. I'd have been surprised to find one there.

I woke up bruised and charged with energy.

I wondered vaguely what she'd told her parents, if anything. I didn't worry about it. I didn't worry about anything at all. There had never been anyone like her in Dead River. In my mood I doubted there was anyone like her anywhere.

I could never have expected her, yet I felt I'd waited for her all my life. Some compensation for all those years of emptiness. It was postcoital euphoria on a massive scale. And more.

I made some coffee and read the morning paper, lying in bed and sipping at the coffee, and every so often the scent of her would waft up from the linen or from me. Unwashed, unshaven, I felt clean as a baby.

It was Saturday, so there was nothing I was pressed to do. It must have taken me two hours to get to the shower. When I came out, dripping, looking for a towel, she was standing by the bed.

"Dry off. We already did that once, remember?"

We spent the day in bed.

Then most of Sunday.

I never did get around to asking her what she'd told her parents. It didn't seem important. Obviously she was handling it one way or another. There was not the slightest hint of tension in her, or of conflict of any kind.

Maybe they knew what they had the same as I did.

Someone special. Someone to whom the rules did not apply. And, like me, asked no questions.

We should have asked.

But there are all kinds of sins, aren't there.

I know them all by now.

I took Monday off. Called in sick. I'd never done it before, not once, so there was no trouble. The rain had passed with the weekend. It was a hot, bright morning—the first of July—and we decided to drive to the beach again.

Steven picked us up in the royal blue Le Baron. He and Kim had already gone on their little shopping spree, so the truck was full of beer and the usual delicacies. I felt glad to be left out of that particular part of it. Steve was in a terrific mood. I wondered aloud if it was the stealing.

"Nah. That's always fun, sure. But my sister's home, see? And guess who's left her little shit of a husband? Young Babs of Radcliffe, that's who. Still all drawly and horsey-looking and completely titless—but free at last. And god! is she ever driving my parents nuts! All she does these past couple of days is give them tears and arrogance and general craziness, and all those other good things that come with shedding a rich partner—and every bit of it's directed at them.

"That's the best part. Because they got her *into* it, you see? They just absolutely *loved* Robert Cowpie Jessup. Not to mention Jessup Laboratories. Oh, over breakfast on the pa-tee-oh she called them leeches. Can you imagine? Leeches! And last night it was pimps.

"I am having a *hell* of a time, I tell you."

"Lots of good feeling between you and the folks, huh?"

"Oh, *tons* of the shit!"

You could have wished it to happen every morning. At least he wasn't driving like a maniac. We took the coast road out at a nice, easy pace for a change. A pleasant little drive in the country with a trunk full of stolen caviar. When we passed the Crouch place he looked at me and grinned.

"I saw lights."

"You saw bullshit."

His mood got us all happy.

Casey said that Kim's straw hat looked like something out of Elvira Madigan by way of Kate Hepburn. Steve picked it up with peasant-girl jokes and farm-girl jokes, most of which centered on Kimberley's ample breasts and thighs, her most conspicuous features. Kim countered with references to the weekend "orgy" between Casey and me, and the whole thing got pretty tasteless, pretty scatological.

We did plenty of laughing. Finally Casey made some comment about the inevitability of a discussion of Kimberley's breasts in any social gathering in which she, Kimberley, was a part, and Kim pulled off the big wide-brimmed hat and stuffed it under the seat and said, okay, you want 'em, you got 'em, and proceeded to peel off the powder blue tank top she was wearing and toss it over her head into the wind.

We watched it flutter down behind us.

We were about a mile from the beach and there she sat, half-naked, her nipples puckering in the breeze.

"Cute," said Casey. "Now what are you gonna wear home?"

Kim giggled. "You worried about it? You shouldn't be. You better wonder what *you're* gonna wear!"

There was a brief struggle behind us.

Moments later Casey's work shirt was observed to waft through the air and drape itself over a roadside cattail.

So now we had two half-naked women in the backseat. The road ahead was deserted. Behind us too. But I kept seeing squad cars pulling us over, officers peering ironically. The girls were laughing so hard their faces flushed red.

"Well, *shit*!" said Steven.

The car began to weave and halt fitfully as he unzipped his jeans and worked them over first one leg and then the other over his sneakers. It took a while but finally he was out of them. I was glad to see he had his briefs.

He placed wallet, belt, and house keys neatly on the seat beside him and handed me a fistful of change and then flipped the pants over his head. We watched them twist away behind us. He looked at me.

"You next."

"Not me."

"Come on."

I tried to look as serious as possible. "You know I hate people to see the catheter."

We made it to our deserted rocky spot on the beach without incident. We ate the odd smorgasbord lunch.

"You know," I said, "I keep wishing for a ham sandwich."

Steve nodded. "Yeah. I got to stop stealing."

Kim halted in the middle of a bite of cheese and cracker. She looked at us and then down at herself.

"What *are* we gonna do about going home?" she said.

I laughed the caviar all over my hand.

The day turned sour.

I was lying on my back, half-asleep, letting the sun bake me. By now my ass was as brown as the rest of me, my modesty having long since gone the way of caution in anything which was related to them. Kim was sitting beside me on a towel rubbing oil into her arms and shoulders. I heard the shout from Steven and the hissing intake of breath from her simultaneously. Both sounds full of sudden fear.

I was up and on my feet in an instant, while Kim was still reacting to what she'd heard.

Part of it I understood immediately.

Steve and Casey had been standing atop the same rock she and I had climbed that first day, that place where gulls had littered the surface with the shells of crabs and oysters. Now she was alone there. Looking down at Steven. In her posture there was a strange tension, not of fear but of anger.

Below her, Steven tried to rise.

There was something disjointed-looking about his limbs, a loss of skill in both arms and legs that made me worry not so much about breakage as concussion.

I ran. I sensed Kim a few steps behind me. When I reached him he was trying to rise again. He fell back heavily on his chest. There was no sand where he was, only stones. It must have hurt him. I heard the breath rush out of his lungs, but that was the only sound from him. I heard us running and that deep whoosh of breath and the crying of gulls. And that was all. A strange, quiet chaos.

I went down beside him and put one arm behind his back to support him, just under his shoulders.

"Relax. Relax."

He looked at me and his eyes were not quite focusing. I saw a small scrape just below the hairline over his right eye. It would swell, but it didn't look too bad. A slight welling up of blood moving slowly to the surface. I looked into his hair for something worse. There was nothing. I guessed he was just shaken. I was damned relieved.

Kim squatted down beside me. I saw her glance to the left of him a little and then heard that intake of breath again. Her face contracted squeamishly. I saw what she was looking at. His left arm was out at a right angle from us, the wrist just sort of dangling. The ball of the thumb was cut pretty badly. There was a steady flow of blood rolling down off his wrist and a flap of skin maybe two inches long pulled back toward the palm of his hand.

"Get me something. Something to press over it and stop the bleeding. Hurry up."

His eyes looked better now, even though the color was still gone from his face. I was pretty sure he'd be all right. He tried to talk to me. The look on his face was one of pure amazement.

"She...she *pushed* me..."

I glared up at her. She hadn't moved. The bright sunlight always made her eyes go oddly transparent. Now it was like staring into two bright cubes of ice.

"You want to tell me about it?"

"No."

"What the fuck is this about, Casey?"

Kim came running back with my T-shirt. I helped her wrap it around his hand and showed her how to press it down.

"Hard," I told her. Then I looked back at Casey.

"I asked you something."

I saw her shoulders relax slightly. Her voice was low, contemptuous. Scary.

"You can go to hell."

She stepped back away from us.

"You both can."

I watched her disappear down the far face of the rock. I covered Kim's hand and helped her press down on Steven's wound. I glanced at Kim. She was totally concentrated on him.

It was only then that I realized I was shaking.

I never did find out what caused it, though I was pretty sure he'd made some moves on her. His mood was just silly enough for him to try.

Nobody talked about it.

We drove home with the girls in the back seat wrapped in towels and the two of us in front. Same as before. Only this time I was driving and Steve was clutching his hand, squeezing my bloody T-shirt to a wound that would take seven stitches once we got back to town.

All the way home nobody said a word. The freeze between Casey and Kim was a palpable thing. You could hardly blame Kim. I was damned mad at her myself. No matter what had gone on up there, it was clear she'd overreacted, to say the very least. And then I kept seeing that cold unconcern of her face while she stared at us. It could have been a concussion. Yet all we got was anger.

You had to wonder. How well did I even know her?

And despite our weekend together, that kept coming up again. I kept wondering how many more surprises there would be like the one today, and whether I really wanted to be around to see them.

I dropped the women off at their respective houses. Then I got a spare pair of pants from my apartment, helped him on with them and took him to Doc Richardson over on Cedar Street. I stood there watching through the injection, the bandaging, the stitching, the swabbing and patching of the head wound while the Doc complained good-naturedly that the times had not been good since Hoover.

By the time we drove back through town Steve was feeling better. I dropped him at his parents' summer house and watched him move slowly up the fieldstone walk, through the white colonial doors.

I didn't see him again for nearly a week.

The next I saw of Kim she was still angry. But you could tell that the bitterness was wearing off some, eroded by understanding. We sat in a booth at Harmon's together drinking Cokes. She, too, suspected Steve had made a move on Casey.

She thought he had reasons, though.

"We're alike, Casey and I. The both of us wear a kind of sign, like one of those sandwich boards. The sign says Sex. Now, I don't figure that's so bad. A lot of women wear it. And plenty of us aren't after anything in particular except some fun, some pleasure, a little give-and-take. I figure that all things being equal, we're just about the best kind of woman there is. A whole lot better than some dried-up and sad-assed type like Steve's sister. Because we can switch it over to love at the drop of hat.

"But sometimes I think that Casey uses it, you know? Like it's some kind of dynamite she has so she can blow loose whatever she wants out of life. And I think that's not so good. Dangerous, even. I know that Steve's wanted her since they were kids, even though he wants me too. But I think I'm good for him, basically. And she isn't.

"Maybe she's good for you—I don't know about that. But not Steve. Not ever. Though every now and then, he keeps trying.

"And I can't help but thinking that it's not good for her, either, to be that way. What's it for, anyway? Pleasure. Pleasure and affection. But for Casey I think it's something else, something it shouldn't be. Like conquest.

"Or hunger."

Eight

"WHAT DO YOU WANT, CASE?"

We were lying in bed at my apartment.

"*What's worth having?*"

Her face was only inches from mine. Her eyes let me down into the depths of her. I slid there gratefully.

"Pleasure.

"Knowledge. Security. I want to own good things, I guess.

Success, eventually. And something astonishing, something that surprises me. Or me, surprising myself."

I didn't question her. I just watched her eyes narrow. She sat up suddenly, catlike in the moonlight.

"Will is worth having. *Power*."

Nine

"HOW GOES IT AMONG THE RICH, STUD?"

Rafferty was in his usual corner place at the bar, near the wall with the old crooked print by Frederic Remington overhead. You could see everybody enter and leave from there and you had a clear view all the way back to the jukebox. The clock on the wall said five-fifteen.

"Air's a little thin at the moment."

I told him about Steven and Casey pushing him. He shook his head and grinned at me.

"Line from some Warren Oates movie. I always remembered it. 'If they didn't have cunts, there'd be a bounty on 'em.'"

He sipped his beer.

"How deep you in?"

"Pretty deep, I guess."

"Too bad you can't just switch tracks. That little blond looks sweet and easy."

"I think she probably is."

"But no banana, huh?"

"Nope."

I ordered a shot of scotch with a beer back from Hank McCarty, the bartender, and he brought it over. My hands were still dusted with a fine brown powder from the saw at the yard. It turned a muddy mahogany when I picked up the frosted glass.

"You got to think about what you're doing here, Danny boy. What the fuck are you doing? You gonna up and marry the girl? Maybe chase her back to Boston or wherever that school of hers is come September? Work a lathe while she picks up her degree?

What are you getting all worried about? Screw her, have fun with her and let it ride."

"Sure."

"I mean it."

"Look, George. I haven't got it all mapped out. Things just happen. You know that."

He looked annoyed. "Yeah, well they can just *un*happen too."

I didn't want to argue. Besides, he was probably right. In a lot of ways I was walking around with blinders on when it came to Casey—no past, no future and a very narrow focus to the present. About the length of one summer. That was okay so long as I knew it was a temporary thing by nature, so long as I was prepared to lose it and then go on.

I wasn't. There was a basic mistake operating and I knew it. I was already half-committed to the girl and I didn't know a thing about her except physical things and what you could deduce in the space of a couple of weeks, some of which wasn't very good. So what was I getting involved in? She was rich, for god's sake. I was her summer playmate. It wouldn't be hard to get pretty annoyed with me myself.

It seemed like a good time to tie one on. I ordered another round for us.

"That's right, get a little sloppy. You'll feel better."

"Do me a favor, George?"

"Sure."

"If she ever pushes *me* off a cliff somewhere, kick the shit out of her?"

"Be glad to."

We drank our beers and watched the Caribou fill up steadily with the after-work crowd. I was always interested to see the mix. Jeans, dirty T-shirts, overalls, business suits from Sears. We got salesmen, fishermen, laborers. A smattering of women. All kinds of people. Bars up here don't cater to a single type of crowd the way they do in the cities. There's not enough clientele for that. Bar life is about as democratic as we get.

"Jim Palmer was in yesterday. We were talking about you."

"Me? I hardly know the guy."

"Well, not about you exactly. I mentioned that your friend had seen lights over at the Crouch place. Jimmie did all the contracting on the place, remember? Anyhow, he says there's nobody there now. So it must have been kids."

"I guess."

"Found out a few things, though."

"Like what?"

He settled back in the high-back chair and sipped the head off a fresh-poured beer.

"Well, for one thing, that doctor left scared."

"Scared?"

"According to Palmer. Says he was up there maybe a month before the old guy left the place, because there was some patch-up that needed doing on the front porch, but the doc wouldn't let him bother with it. Had to go down into the basement instead to seal up a hole in the wall. Big hole. Said it looked as though somebody's been whacking away at it with a sledgehammer. He couldn't figure it. Said the doc was a pretty weird guy. But he could understand him wanting it patched up again. The draft was fierce.

"In the basement?"

"Sure. Palmer says that in a couple of places the foundation's sitting right beside some open spaces in the seawall. Tunnels. Erosion or whatever. Said that whole stretch of coast is honeycombed with 'em. So you open up one of those spaces and the wind runs right in from the sea. Anyway, he closed it up. I told him about our little excursion out that way when we were kids."

"I still don't get it. The draft was what scared him? What was he, afraid of summer colds?"

"Jimmie says he doesn't really know what it was. Just that he was already talking about leaving. Maybe he was afraid the whole house was going to slide down into those tunnels some day. You know, the way they go out in California. But that cellar is sunk in solid rock. He had no problem there. No, he couldn't figure what it was."

"Ben and Mary's ghosts."

"Could be."

"You sound like you've got more."

"I do. Did you know they were imbeciles?"

"You mean crazy."

"No. Imbeciles. It's a pretty ugly story, actually. It seems that when the bank called in that mortgage money they had a town meeting about it. See, all Ben knew was farming, and he was pretty bad at that. But there was no possibility of either of them doing anything else for a living. So somebody came up with the bright idea of having the town pay off the mortgage. It was only a little over a thousand. And they figured it would cost them a whole lot more than that just in bookkeeping and whatnot to keep them on the dole for thirty, maybe forty years than it would to pay off and let them keep the place.

"But the upshot was that somebody got cheap about it, I guess, so the proposal was turned down. And it looked like Dead River was going into the social welfare business for a while. Very exciting. But then, of course, Ben and Mary disappeared and saved everybody the trouble."

"Imbeciles, huh?"

"Total morons. Ben couldn't read and couldn't write. He could handle a plow and Mary could wring a chicken's neck and that was about the whole of it. Now, where do you go if you're that stupid? That's the next question. How do you manage disappearing?"

"You could die."

"That would be the easy way, yes."

"Or just wander off. A county or two down the line."

"Or you could do what my boss did and open a garage."

"You could do that."

He pushed the empty glass away from him and his smile was sly, a little boozy. His hands waved apparitions in the space around us.

"Or maybe you just go back into the caves," he said. "And forget about us entirely. Maybe you live off fish and weeds and spend your days listening to the gulls and the wind off the sea, and you don't come out, not ever."

"Jesus, Rafferty."

I felt a slight prickling at the base of my neck. He looked at me and the smile grew even more cagey and ironic, like a cop in a morgue uncovering a cadaver.

"That doctor. I wonder if he ever heard dogs barking."

Ten

I DECIDED A FEW DAYS LATER that Rafferty's sense of humor was getting sort of surreal.

Maybe it was the tourists turning up so early this year because of the good weather—they could breed a bitter irony in you made up of easy money and bad manners, privilege and your own unquestionable need. One day I saw a fat man in sunglasses and Bermuda shorts walking by the Caribou carrying fishing tackle and drinking eggnog right out of the carton.

It was pretty sickening.

Then that same day Rafferty tells me this story about some woman over in Portland who was suing an Italian spaghetti sauce company for mental anguish because she opened a can of marinara and found a woman's finger inside a rubber glove pointing fingernail-up at her.

The next day he had another one.

He'd read it in the paper.

The body of a night watchman had been found in a hogpen at a meat-packing firm on the South Side of Chicago. It had been partly eaten by the hogs. There were hundreds of them in the pen, and the guy's face and abdomen were in pretty bad shape. But here's the kicker.

His clothes were hanging neatly on a nearby fence.

Rafferty made some nasty obvious comments about going after pigs in the dark.

So I thought he was getting strange lately.

But maybe it wasn't him entirely.

Sometimes I think there's something just hanging in the air, and almost everybody reacts to it. Don't ask me why. Sometimes it's real and vital, like when JFK was shot. And sometimes it's completely unimportant, like pennant fever. Sometimes, like the recession, it goes on and on, and you get so you hardly even notice it. Maybe Dead River was getting a touch of that.

And I'll tell you why I think it wasn't just Rafferty.

There was us.

The stealing. All the dumb, reckless things we were doing. The business with Steven. The stolen car. There was my own blind, self-destructive urge to follow along, no matter what kind of ridiculous thing they were into doing.

There was a statue of a mounted revolutionary soldier in the town square. One night we painted the horse's balls bright red. Two nights later we painted them blue.

We were sitting on the beach one afternoon, and Casey was in the water—it had grown warmer by then, though it was still too cold for me. Steve was still nursing his torn hand, so he'd stayed home that day, so there was just me and Kim sitting there alone together, watching her, and we got to talking about Steve's accident—we called it an accident now—in a boring sort of way. The stitches, when they were due out, to what degree he could flex the damn thing. We were remembering how it had been that day without ever once coming close to the heart of the thing, which was why she'd done it. We skirted that.

But I guess it made her think of this other story, which I'm mentioning here because it bears upon what I was saying about something being in the air by then, something made of god knows what and disgorging itself on Dead River.

Kim was only a little girl at the time, she said.

There was a family living next door to her who had a

teenage daughter. An only child. Not a pretty girl or terribly smart either. Sort of ordinary. A little unfriendly and sullen.

Anyway, for her birthday—her seventeenth—her parents gave her two presents, a car and a Doberman puppy. Probably, Kim said, she was unpopular at school, and the one gift—the car—was to make her more popular, while the other gift was to console her if it didn't work out.

But the girl did love the puppy.

Both her parents had jobs, so the dog was home alone most of the time during the day, and Kim remembered the girl's car roaring into the driveway each afternoon at three-thirty and the girl racing up the steps while the dog barked loudly and scratched at the screen door. Then there would be a lot of jumping and squealing and hugging, which even as a kid Kim found pretty disgusting. And finally there would be a very big puppy tearing crazily around their own and Kim's property.

This happened every day.

Then one day there was none of it. The girl came home and there was no barking and no scratching at the door. Just silence. Kim was playing in the yard as usual and noticed that something was wrong. They'd all gotten pretty used to the dog by then. So she watched. The girl went inside.

A few minutes later the girl came out holding the puppy and raced for the car. She put the dog inside and quickly drove away. That was all Kim saw. The rest she heard about later.

When the girl got home the puppy was in the kitchen, choking. There was something caught in its throat. So she bundled it up and drove to the vet. The vet took a look at the dog and told her to wait outside. She did, for a while. But then the waiting started to get to her so she decided to drive on home, and asked the nurse to call her when the doctor was through.

She was only in the house a few minutes when the phone rang. It was the vet. She said the dog was all right and asked her if she was home alone. She said she was. He told her to get out of the house right away, to go stand on the lawn or on the street. The police, he said, would be over right away.

She was not to ask questions. She was just to leave as fast as possible.

They found her waiting on the front lawn, walking in circles, confused and worried. Two squad cars emptied four officers into her house.

Upstairs, hiding in her father's closet, they found a man with a shirt wrapped tight around a bleeding index finger. Or what was left of it. I guess the dog had proven itself a good watchdog but a clumsy eater. He'd taken the intruder's finger off at the knuckle and swallowed it whole. And that was what was lodged there in his throat.

"I'm supposed to believe that?"

"Absolutely."

Two finger stories in one week, I thought.

"If you don't believe me, ask Casey. The girl used to babysit for her brother."

"*Her brother*?"

I guess I jumped on that one a little.

"Sure. You...you knew about her brother, didn't you?"

"Yes and no."

She knew she'd made a mistake. I watched her get more and more uncomfortable, trying to figure how to handle it. Finally she said, "Well, you can ask Casey about Jean Drummond. She'll tell you."

"Talk to me about her brother, Kim."

She considered it. I had the feeling that there was something there she thought I ought to know. I knew she liked me. I remembered her warning about Casey over Cokes that day. Loyalties, though. They die hard.

"I'd...rather not. That's Casey's business."

"Not mine? Not even a little?"

"I didn't say that."

"So? Should I ask her about it, Kimberley?"

She paused. "Maybe you should. I don't know. It depends."

"On what."

"On how well you need to know her, I guess."

"Suppose that's a lot?"

She sighed. "Then ask. *Ask* her, for god's sake. Jesus! I can't hold your goddamn hand for you."

She stood and walked away from me into the shallows. As far as I knew it was the first time she'd gone into the water all summer. I called out to her.

"*You won't like it.*"

She turned around and looked at me. She spoke quietly.

"Neither will you."

Eleven

The opportunity to ask about her brother came along two nights later.

I think I remember everything there is to remember about that night. The smell of fresh-cut grass on her lawn, the warmth of the air—its exact temperature—the scent of her hair moving toward me and then away on the flow of breeze through the open windows as we drifted along in the car, the feel of damp earth under me later and the smell of that too, the long empty silences, crickets, night birds, her awful shallow breathing.

I remember every bit of it, because that night put all the rest in motion. And the next day was Saturday, and the next night was Saturday night. And I've never looked at Saturdays the same way since. Maybe you'll find that hard to believe. But you weren't there.

You don't carry it around with you like a sackful of cinders.

Like I say, you weren't there.

~~~~~~~~~~

I'd taken the day off again and this time the boss wasn't happy with me at all. I was "ill" again. McGregor wasn't stupid.
~~~~~~~~~~

You only had to look at Casey once or twice to know what was keeping me away.

I was endangering the job. I didn't care.

We drove to Campobello for the day to see the Roosevelt summer home. We were the only ones there, so the guide gave us special attention. Steven, whose hand was still wrapped in bandages, found it all a bit hard to take.

"There's an awful lot of wicker."

He was right as far as I was concerned. Nice house, big, but otherwise nothing special. The guide was a lot more impressed than any of us were. But that was her job. She was a nice old woman and you didn't want to insult her. Except for Steve, who kept wandering off impatiently by himself, we followed her and nodded attentively.

It was a relief to get outside, though.

"Thank god," said Steve as we piled back into the car. "How do tourists stand themselves, anyway?"

"They still believe in education," Casey said.

Steve nodded. "Self-improvement."

"History."

We stopped for a drink at the Caribou on the way home. Hank always served us, though I'm sure he knew they were underage. I suppose he needed the business.

It was still early and the after-work crowd hadn't arrived yet, so we had the place nearly to ourselves. Steve played some Elvis and Jerry Lee on the jukebox. All the drinks were the usual—scotch with beer back for me, Bloody Marys for Casey and Steve and a tequila sunrise for Kimberley. We finished one round and ordered another. And that was when the disagreement started.

We'd planned to drive to Lubec that night to listen to a local band there, one Kim happened to like. Steve and I were agreeable. But Casey hadn't committed herself. And now it turned out that there was a movie she wanted to see over in Trescott. It was nothing to me either way, but Steve got annoyed with her.

"Anything you want, Casey. Don't mind me."

She swirled the ice in her Bloody Mary, oblivious to his irony.

"Fine."

"You go to your movie and we'll go see the band."

"All right."

"What about you, Dan?"

He was pointing his finger at me again. He was using the bandaged hand and it was sort of funny-looking but I didn't dare laugh. I kept it straight.

"I guess I'll go to the movie."

"That's fine too."

You could see he was ready to walk out in one of his ten-minute sulks. He still had half a drink left, but he got up off his stool.

"Sit down, Steven," said Kimberley. "We can all get together tomorrow night. Relax."

It didn't really take. He still wanted to march off on us, you could tell. It was all display. Competitive, possessive and pretty silly. By tomorrow he'd have forgotten all about it. In this kind of contest of wills with Casey he never won anyway. You wondered why he bothered.

But he sat, and he finished his drink. And then stalked off, without a word or a smile for any of us. I turned to Kimberley.

"Are you going to get more of this tonight? Maybe you ought to come along with us."

"No, he'll be fine. He'll walk it off now. Besides, I'm the one who wants to hear the band, remember?"

Casey was expected home for dinner. So I ate alone at the diner, something very rubbery they had the guts to call a steak, and then drove out to her place and waited. I didn't like going inside unless I had to. The few times I had, Casey's mother had been very uncomfortable. I had the distinct sense that she thought her daughter was slumming. She was a fluttery, mousy thing, and I didn't like her much. Casey's looks came from her father. As for him, he made *me* uncomfortable.

I was about to find out why.

The street was so quiet you could almost feel the dusk turn to dark around you like a slag of fog descending. I heard crickets, and somebody dropped a pan a few doors down. I heard kids shouting somewhere out of sight down the block, playing some game or other, and a mother's voice calling one of them home for dinner.

Casey was late.

After a while I heard voices raised inside their house. I'd never had the illusion that they were a happy family. On the other hand, I'd never heard them fighting, either.

I checked my watch. Ten minutes after seven. The movie started at eight. It would take us half an hour to drive to Trescott. It was going to be tight, but we'd still have a little leeway.

I waited. I didn't mind waiting. There was no temptation to turn on the radio. I'd always liked the evening quiet of Dead River. It was one thing the town had to offer, a kind of gentle cooling of the spirit that comes along with the cooling of the land. The summer nights were almost worth the winter nights, when you suffered, housebound, through the cold. You could almost feel the stars come out, without seeing them.

I was eased back, sitting low in the seat, dreaming.

I jumped when I heard the door slam.

There was no light on in front of the house, so it was hard to see her face at first as she came towards the car, but I could tell from something in her walk, in the way she moved, that she was upset. Her movements were always so controlled and confident, made up of loose and well-toned muscle. But now I saw a rough abruptness about her that I wasn't used to. She pulled the door open on the passenger side.

"*Drive*."

She launched herself into the seat. Her voice seemed thicker, angry.

"What's up?"

"Please just drive."

"You still want the movie?"

"Yes. I don't care. Anywhere. Fuck it!"

"Easy, Case."

I think she took a good five years off the life of my car door. My ears rattled in tandem with the window. I started the car.

"Easy."

She turned to me, and something took a dive in the pit of my stomach. Those lovely pale eyes gleamed at me. I'd never seen her cry before. I started to reach for her, to comfort her.

"*Please!*"

She was begging.

Casey, begging. I couldn't quite believe it at first.

I did what she asked. I drove.

I don't know where we went.

The outskirts of town for a while, then up and down the main streets. Then out of town again.

I tried to get her to talk about it, but she shut me up with a look so painful that I kept my own eyes fixed to the road ahead after that and gave her the long quiet that was clearly all she wanted from me and all I had to give. I felt her body shaking gently and knew she was crying. It astonished me that anything could happen in that colorless, moneyed, lifeless household that could possibly make her cry. It astonished me that she should cry at all, I think. The command was gone, the toughness melted away, and beside me was a woman like any other. And even though I liked that toughness and that command, I realized I'd been waiting a long time to see this, to see what was underneath.

It was good to know I could help her just by being there. I felt oddly comforted. I'd never cared for her more.

It was quite a moment.

I remember we'd turned onto Northfield Avenue when I felt her straighten up beside me. Out of the corner of my eye I watched her wipe the tears off her face. It was a single harsh gesture with the fingertips of both hands. I heard her sniffling back the mucus and heard her clear her throat. We turned to one another at the same time. For me it was just a glance before I had to look back to the road again. But I felt her stare on me long after that, measuring me somehow.

When she spoke, her voice was gentle, but I sensed that she'd turned a corner again, and what lay beneath it was not. I'd seen a crack in the wall, no more than that. Her voice ran drifts of ectoplasm over me like the thin, strong lines of a spider.

"I want to go back."

"You want me to take you home?"

"Please. Yes."

"All right."

We weren't far from there. We drove in silence. I turned onto her street and noticed a pothole in the road I hadn't seen when we'd passed it before. It seemed out of place on that one good street in all Dead River.

I parked across from her house and put the pickup in parking gear. It rumbled: the idle was running high again. I put my arm across the seat and turned to ask her if she wouldn't like to tell me about it before she went inside again. I wanted to know. It wasn't just curiosity. She was putting me through some very fast changes. I felt she'd cut me off again, done it quickly and thoroughly, and I wanted back in. She opened the curbside door.

"Wait for me here."

She closed the door carefully, quietly.

I turned off the car and watched her.

She crossed the street and walked up the field-stone path that cut the lawn in two and led up to the porch. There were low shrubs planted in a rock garden roughly as deep as the porch on either side. They ascended in height, the symmetry almost too neat to please the eye. She stopped in front of the first step and looked off to her left. She was looking for something on the ground.

Now what the hell?

She took a few steps to the left and kept on looking. I had

the ridiculous momentary impression that it was night crawlers she was after. That we were going fishing. She bent down into the garden and took something up in each hand, seeming to weigh them before she stood again.

From that point on her movements were completely economical. The Casey I was used to, and even more so.

It was clear that she knew exactly what she was doing. She took three steps backward onto the lawn and looked up into the left front window. There was a light burning inside from a floor lamp. I tried to remember the layout of the house, and I thought it would have to be the den, her father's workroom.

There is something terrible to me about the sound of breaking glass.

I remember we had a cat when I was a kid who woke us all one night by knocking a cheap cut-glass vase off the kitchen table. I was on my feet and into the kitchen so fast that I wasn't fully awake when I got there. With the result that the sole of my foot took seven or eight stitches.

That's how it was this time too.

I think my hand was on the ignition as soon as her rock went crashing through the window. I think the car was in drive and my foot on the brake before the shattering sound even left my ears. Part of it was instinct, part of it self-preservation.

It was her house. But I had the feeling it would be my ass.

My throat felt constricted.

"Jesus!" I yelled. "Come on!"

Somehow I couldn't get her attention.

She was still moving in that same determined way across the fieldstone path and then across the right side of her lawn, ignoring me. I knew instantly what she was doing, where she was going. I knew it like I knew how my head would hurt if you hit it with a hammer. There would be no stopping her. Calling out would only make it worse. The sound of breaking glass had been so loud I half expected to see porch lights go on all along the street. But everything was still quiet. As she marched across the lawn and over a macadam driveway to the house next door.

I looked back to her place. My hands were sweating on the steering wheel. I saw her father framed in the window. He had just come through the doorway and was standing there in perfect profile, staring down at the damage, at all the broken glass I imagined winking up at him from the floor.

He turned slowly toward the window and pressed his palms carefully to the windowsill and looked out. He looked to the right and then to the left, and then he looked at me.

I had to turn away.

There was too much sadness there, too much guilt in me.

I heard another crash. Louder than before. She had put the second rock through the right front window of the house next door.

I didn't ask myself why. I knew why. There would be questions now, plenty of them. Her father would be answering some of them.

There was shouting inside. A woman. A man. Casey was straightening up, recovering the follow-through. A slab of glass came drifting down off the top sill like the blade of a guillotine, hit the bottom sill and shattered. The shouting sounded almost hysterical to me.

I watched her walk back to the car. She took her time.

There was a moment when I almost left her there. I glanced back to her place and saw that her father was gone from the window. The porch lights went on. Soon he would be standing there. I leaned out to her.

"Get in, goddamn you!"

Sympathy can turn so quickly. Just add fear. Stir.

By the time she was back in the car I was burning. Burning and scared. I had just enough control left not to gun the thing to get away from there. We slid away from the curb nice and slowly.

See no evil, hear no evil.

I wondered if anybody was buying it but me.

I wanted to hit her.

I wanted to slap her so bad my shoulders twitched. I

wouldn't even look at her. I kept thinking how she'd involved me, how she'd done this *to me*. Not just to the people next door or to her parents for whatever idiot reason, but to me. I hadn't done anything. I hadn't asked for it.

Had I?

All kinds of things went through my head. I felt like opening the door on her side and giving her a push. Never mind that the car was moving. Fuck her. If she could do that to me. Just fuck her.

I drove two blocks under the most careful, most frantic control of my life, absolutely boiling inside, and then hit it hard and went looking for the highway.

I hit sixty on the quiet streets of Dead River and pushed it up to seventy-five on the coast road. The road was not nearly good enough for seventy-five. Neither was the pickup. I realized what I was doing and pulled over.

I was going to get us killed.

I cut the engine, cut the lights. We sat there in the deep black of empty night on the shoulder of a bad road with no one around but the crickets and the frogs, and I had not lost an ounce of my delicious anger. I held out as long as I could, hoping she'd say something to make it all right again, knowing in my heart that there was nothing she could say, not now. And then I groped for where I knew her shirt would be and pulled her over with both my hands and shook her like a rag doll, bounced her against the car seat while she whimpered to me to please stop and I told her to go to hell and felt the shirt tear along the sides of my big, happy fists.

"You don't *understand*!"

She was crying again but this time I didn't care. It didn't mean a thing. She couldn't touch me. I shook her until I felt the shirt go at the shoulder too and then that was no good to me so I slid my hand into her hair and shook her that way.

"You sonovabitch! *You don't understand*!"

Then suddenly I had a tearstained screeching little bomb on my hands.

Twelve

I'VE TOLD YOU SHE WAS ALL MUSCLE.

Well, we came close to taking out the front seat in that pickup of mine.

I could barely see her and she could barely see me, so there was a lot of inadvertent pain for both of us. One of us broke the rearview mirror. Somebody put a dent in the radio as big as an apple.

When it finally wore down for us the palms of my hands were wet with her tears and the musty smell of them filled the car as she sobbed into my shoulder, great mangled racking sounds that tore what was left of my anger to shreds and left me holding her, stroking her, wondering how in hell it had come to this, anyway.

"Just hold on to me, huh?"

Her voice was very small against me. She sniffled, laughed a little.

"I...I think I've got a screw loose somewhere, you know? So please just...hold on?"

I did hold her.

And then a little later I heard her sigh.

"God, I'm fucked up!"

"You want to tell me about it?"

She laughed again. It was weighted with sadness.

"No."

"Tell me anyhow."

For a moment she was very still. My hand found the warm bare flesh of her shoulder where I'd torn the shirt. Her breathing was calmer and more even now.

"He hasn't done anything for a long time now. I'd almost forgiven him. Both of us."

She paused, thought a moment. Her voice turned colder.

"No, I hadn't. That's a lie."

"Who? Who are we talking about?"

"My father."

She turned her head away from me slightly so that it rested just below my shoulder and stared out through the windshield. Clouds had parted for the moon again just moments before and now I saw snail tracks of tears across her cheeks, bathed in cool white light, dissolving the tan into something pale and famished-looking.

"He drinks. A lot. You're not supposed to do that when you're vice-president of a bank. So he drinks at home where there's nobody there but us to see.

"My mother would go out. Clubs and meetings and all that, the kind of thing that's expected of a wife in...her position. Because he couldn't manage his end of it. Get him around liquor, and he's drunk. So he stayed in. With us, me and Jimmie, my little brother. Maybe she just wanted to get away from him. I don't know.

"He's not a bad man. He's not mean. Even when he's drunk, he's not mean. Just weak, and foolish. She's very smart. Intolerant, and disappointed, I guess. They should never have married at all. But where she comes from, you get married. You just do."

She glanced at me once and then looked away, shaking her head.

"I'm not doing so good at this."

"Go on."

"When I was thirteen...I guess you could say he raped me."

I waited. I could feel something clog in my throat. I think I'd half expected it. I felt the sudden press of the inevitable. It was as though the car sat underneath a bell jar and we were in a perfect vacuum, with everything extraneous sucked out of it and us except this one moment in time, this one event.

Figure this if you can:

It was then that she seduced me utterly.

I waited. I don't think I so much as blinked. Perhaps a car went by, playing over us with its headlights. I know I saw her very clearly.

"I was in the tub. I still liked baths then.

"We were never very big on privacy. I'd left the door open. I looked up and saw him standing there, and I knew he was drunk. You could always tell. He looked bad. Very bad. I wasn't angry. I...felt sorry for him. I watched him looking at me and I didn't yell and for a while I didn't move or say a word. He'd seen me naked before, but this was...different. I was already a woman by then. I *knew*. I really knew. And I felt bad for him.

"I got up and wrapped a towel around me and walked past him. He didn't touch me. He didn't say anything. I went into my bedroom and closed the door. I remember looking into the mirror for a long, long time.

"I read for a while until I got sleepy and then I went to bed. I could hear him rattling around downstairs in the kitchen. I guess he was drinking some more. But I couldn't sleep. I'd get close and then I'd drift back and I'd hear him again.

"How can I say this? I...*wanted* him to come in. I used to think I'd willed him there. He was so obviously, so terribly unhappy. And I..."

I watched the tears come, watched her fight them to submission before they could take hold of her again.

"...and I loved him. He was my father. He'd never harmed me. And at the same time I was scared...

"I heard his footsteps on the stairs and then the door opened and then he was next to me on the bed, and he was making these sounds and he smelled of whiskey. The smell was bad and the sounds were bad, like someone hurt and frightened. His hands felt so much bigger than I thought they would.

"He stroked my hair and my cheek. He put his hand on my breast. I was wearing pyjamas. He pulled the bottoms off me. I was scared, the way he looked. I asked him to stop. I told him I was sorry, like a little girl who'd been bad. 'I'm sorry,' I said, over and over. I was crying by then. But he kept on touching me. He wasn't hurting me but I was scared, really scared, and I started yelling for him to stop and yelling that I'd tell, I'd tell my mother, and over and over saying I was sorry..."

"So then Jimmie came into the room. Rubbing his eyes. A dumb little kid, eight years old, half-asleep, wondering what all the commotion's about. And there's my father with his pants half-off, and there's his sister bare-assed in bed with Daddy's hand between her legs, and there's blood...all over the sheets, all over my legs. Blood I've just seen for the first time now.

"He ran out of there so fast it scared me worse than I already was, and my father, I remember he just groaned like I'd hurt him bad or something, only it was worse than that, an awful shuddery sound. But he rolled off me. And I...I went after Jimmie.

"We had a little dog. Just a mutt. He was Jimmie's dog but everybody loved him. And we had a staircase in the house just like the one in this one. And the hall was dark. Jimmie...he didn't see the dog lying by the stairs. I ran for him but he went down...and the rest is all just sounds for me. The dog yelping. My father screaming behind me. Jimmie falling down the stairs. And then something loud and wet like if you dropped a...melon. I guess I passed out.

"Jimmie died in a coma. My mother knew everything by then. We got rid of the dog. You just couldn't have him around anymore. My father was sober for about a year, all told..."

She leaned back hard against the seat, exhausted.

I watched her awhile, saying nothing, wondering if she was more comprehensible to me now, wondering if it helped anything.

"And tonight?"

She was silent for a moment, and then she laughed. In the laugh you could see how some of the toughness was made.

"Just now my father, who I suppose has had a couple martinis, had the temerity to put his hands on my shoulders and kiss me on the cheek."

She looked at me and her eyes held that same indifferent cruelty I'd seen that day at the beach, looking down at Steven from that rock, naked and terrible.

"He doesn't touch me. Not ever. I touch him if I feel like it, but nothing else is acceptable. And every time he forgets that, I make him pay. Every time."

I knew a girl once who was rumored to have slept with her father. A local girl. She was a pinched, starved little thing with frightened eyes who held her books tight to her chest and ran on spindly legs from class to class like something vast and evil was always in pursuit. Sitting next to me now was the opposite of her, tempered maybe in the same waters but unbroken, raw and splendid with physical health and power. This one had turned the tables, pursuing the pursuer with a ferocity that probably would have amazed that other girl, but that she would have understood thoroughly.

I wondered, though. I'd met the man. To me he was just a shadow. Insubstantial, insignificant. And I wondered if in that place within where we're all blind and dumb to ourselves, the cat wasn't chasing its own flayed and miserable tail.

"Let's drive," she said.

I started the car. Since we'd met, how many times had she said that now? *Let's drive. Let's just drive.* It never mattered where. Slice a fissure of black macadam through time.

Drive me.

Orders from the lost to the superfluous.

And I think I saw, glimpsed, where I fit in then. Where Kim and Steve fit in too.

We were just diversions, really. Bodies of water suitable for a brief immersion. I diverted her into passion. If we were lucky, orgasm. Steve and Kim into something that looked like friendship but was probably more like continuity, habit. Company. There was nothing—not even her father or the memory of her brother—between Casey and Casey. Not anymore. She'd expelled everybody else. Maybe it's like that for all of us. I don't know.

I know we all are lonely. Locked off from one another in some fundamental secrecy. But some of us declare war and some of us don't.

This isn't a value judgment upon Casey. I'm sure she had her reasons, that for her it was the only strategy. I don't think she came to it out of any elemental cruelty.

But war is still death. Death made unselective and infectious. Tonight she'd repelled a minor invasion. But it had cost her. A piece of her father, a piece of me. And something of herself too. She was dying. She would always be. Casey could survive, but not intact. There were some rules she couldn't break. And the best of her was as vulnerable as the worst.

I drove. Silence thick around us. Eyes fixed to the road in the headlights as though eyes and lights were one and the same.

I knew she did not want sympathy. I knew she'd talked it through and then had wrested the confidence back from me again and thrust it away inside her. In the morning there would be broken windows. The only evidence that it had ever happened.

I drove. Slow through the little towns and back roads and fast—very fast—over the long rolling hills between. We saw a doe frozen in the headlights along the side of the road. The clouds had cleared away and the moon was bright, the sky filled with stars. I felt like I had a destination, a purpose, but of course I didn't. The purpose was just the feel of motion, the car cutting through the night.

We went up through Eastport and Perry and Pembroke, turned south and drove to Whiting. I was hardly aware of the circle moving in on itself. To me they were just towns, all familiar and alike.

It was two in the morning when we started heading back to Dead River. The roads were empty. We hadn't seen a car for miles. At West Lubec we went over a wooden bridge. We passed a little country church, bone white and bleak with disrepair.

"Stop here," she told me.

Thirteen

SHE GOT OUT OF THE CAR AND WALKED toward the church. I followed her. Beneath the bridge the crickets and frogs were a single texture of percussive sound.

The door was fastened with a single Yale lock. Perhaps there was nothing inside worth stealing.

The white paint was chipped and flaking. She pulled a long strip of it off the door. The Yale lock was rusted. I flipped it with my thumb.

"Sad shape."

"I sort of like it."

We peered in through the window. It was too dark to see much there. A row of hardwood benches. In the distance, outlined by moonlight, what looked like a small raised altar. We walked around back.

"It's old. A hundred years or more, I'd bet."

She wasn't listening. She grabbed my arm.

"Look."

Behind the church and off to the left there were about thirty upright stones—broken, chipped, eroded—behind a low wrought-iron fence.

"Come on."

She took my hand. We walked among the leaning headstones. We each took out packs of matches and read the inscriptions. On some of them there wasn't enough left to read.

Beloved wife of. Beloved daughter to.

Most seemed to have died in the mid-to-late 1800s. A lot of them were women, and young.

"Childbirth," she said.

"Lydia, wife of John Pritchett. She died in child-bed December thirtieth, 1876, in the twenty-third year of her age. Sarah, daughter of Mr. Johnathan Clagg, wife to William Lesley, who died thirteenth of June 1856, in the eighteenth year of her age. That one too, maybe."

There was one that made us laugh. *Elisha Bowman. Died March 21st, 1865. Aged 33 yrs, 1m, 14d. He believed that nothing but the success of the Democratic party would ever save this Union*. There was some good carving on the headstone.

I lit another match and looked it over. A skeleton inside a circle described by a snake swallowing its own tail. The skeleton was grinning. In one hand it held an apple, in the other, an hourglass. Beneath, two bats. Above, two seraphim. Pretty elaborate, I thought, for a failed optimist, dead at thirty-three.

After a while I found one I liked even better. *Here lies the body of Bill Trumbell,* it read, *dead in 1829. Been here and gone. Had a good time*.

Strange how even laughter has a hush to it in a place like that at night. You talk as though there's somebody around. And maybe there is. A hundred-year parade of mourners, for one thing, some of them standing there just as you are now in the moonlight, thinking about the past and loved ones gone. The aura of last rights given among simple people who still believed in god and the devil and the Democrats.

And the people underground.

Dead of poison and measles and gunshot wounds and hard birthing. The restless dead. You can hear them in the rustling leaves, see them in the leaning slabs of stone.

"A virgin. Look."

I walked to where she was.

The stone was down, fallen heavily against the smaller one beside it. Casey was bending low, a match about to burn her fingertips. I blew it out and lit another.

We read the inscription. *Here lyes the remains of Elizabeth Cotton, Daughter of the Reverend Samuel Cotton late of Sandwich Mass., who died a Virgin October 12, 1797, aged 36. Who hath not ever sinned*. It was the oldest stone we'd seen there.

"Poor lady. Maybe she should have met up with Bill Trumbell over there."

"I think it's very sad," she said.

The match went out and she lit a third one. An angel was carved over the inscription, almost weathered away. The stone was rough, pitted by wind and rain. You could see the slight indentation where the stone had uprooted itself, just a shallow dip in the soil by now. I stood up.

"Let's go."

"Wait."

The match flickered away again. I'd been working so hard to read that for a moment everything went black. Then my eyes adjusted to the moonlight.

Casey gleamed in it.

The pullover blouse lay beside her. She was naked to the waist, her breasts and belly and shoulders naked, and she was reaching for me.

"Oh no."

"Yes."

"No, Casey."

"Come on. Right on top of Elizabeth Cotton, virgin."

"It's silly."

"You think so?"

I watched her lean back and slip the jeans down off her thighs, the thin panties folding away with them, graceful as a snake shedding its skin. She tossed them away and lay back against the cool earth, reached over her head and took one side of the headstone of Elizabeth Cotton in each hand. In the moonlight her tanned flesh looked unnaturally pale. She smiled at me and moved against the stunted grass.

"Come on. I want you in me."

Just a whisper. Like a razor sliding through paper. It seemed to force the blood through my veins and trigger a heavy pounding in my chest. I wanted her. With all I'd seen of her tonight, I wanted her worse than ever. I felt like a man in a life jacket who finally accepts the water's numbing cold. This was hers. Pure Casey. Undiluted. In the Middle Ages, they'd have burned her at the stake.

I took off my clothes and stood there a moment, naked, looking down at her, watching myself rise. Amazed a little.

Then I went into her.

I went in hard, tickled by perversity. The smell of damp musty earth suddenly strong around us. I pumped at her until her cool skin grew warm again and then moved her violently on top of me, exchanging places with her—the ground, the old crumbled bones beneath my arched back and thighs.

She reached down. Her fingers clawed the damp soil. She took up a handful and ground it against my chest. I felt a sudden all-enveloping chill. She leaned over me and grasped the headstone in both hands again and I rose up high to meet her.

I looked up into a face that was already trembling on the near side of orgasm, past the blind-seeming eyes, and glimpsed myself as though reflected in some dream image as clouds drifted by the moon. I saw us as though from above, locked together, clashed in need. The headstone behind me. I saw huge dead hands reach up out of the churning earth and pull us down.

As she screamed, I felt those hands on me.

Broken stalagmite fingers. On my shoulders. On my neck. Lightly clutching.

Cold and sweating, I came too. And screamed along with her. While the hands receded. Tendrils of smoky mist, climbing back into the soil.

"My god!"

I heard my own nervous laughter.

"You too, huh?"

"You were moving at me right up out of the ground. I was fucking a dead man!"

I felt her shudder. Her body sparkled with beads of sweat.

"God! Kiss me. Kiss me easy."

It was very soft and warm. For a moment I felt the strangeness clear a tiny space for us, like stepping into a dense fog and watching it swirl away around your feet. I felt her cool breasts brush my chest, smelled the rich natural perfume of her damp hair. She was Casey, just Casey. Slightly nuts but that was all.

I still lay inside her.

Like the dead, it would take only a little imagination to get me to rise again.

I broke the kiss and gently lifted her away.

"No more?"

"I think we've educated old Liz Cotton."

I stood up and pulled on my clothes. She sat still a moment fingering a blade of grass, the picture of healthy life amid all those twisted shapes of tombstones. Suddenly I heard the crickets and the frogs again. They'd been there all along, but I was elsewhere.

She got dressed. The last thing she put on was her pullover blouse. She tugged it on over her head and then thought of something. While it was still around her neck she kissed the palm of her hand and pressed it to the headstone of Elizabeth Cotton.

"Somebody had to," she said.

We walked back through the cemetery to the church. Neither of us spoke. I glanced at the padlock on the door and shook my head.

"You know why I was so mad before? Back at your house. You know why I hit you?"

"The windows. The broken windows. I don't blame you."

"No. Just partly that."

"What else?"

I pointed to the padlock.

"Look at that. It's ridiculous. A Yale lock wouldn't keep out a determined ten-year-old."

"So?"

"So I know. Remember I told you there was one other brush with the law?"

"Yes?"

The blue eyes glittered at me.

"Breaking and entering. I was fourteen years old. It was no big thing. A lot of scare tactics at the police station, that was all. And bad times with my mom and dad for a while.

"A lock like this?"

"God, no! You wouldn't want a lock like this on anything bigger than a shed. That's what I mean. No, this was a house over on Maple. Properly closed for the winter. I went through a window on the ground floor. Wandered around awhile. Somebody saw my flashlight through the living-room window."

"But why? What were you doing? Stealing?"

"Good thing I wasn't, or I wouldn't have gotten off with just a warning. No matter how many cops my dad knew. No, that was the weird part. I didn't go there to steal.

"When they got there—the cops, I mean—I'd just been sitting in the living room, in this big old easy chair, wondering what the people were like. And smoking a cigarette. I'd almost forgotten that. I guess I did steal something. The cigarette. From a tired old pack on the kitchen table."

We walked to the car and I thought about it. I hadn't thought about it for years. And I'm not sure I'd ever asked myself exactly what the point had been.

"I don't know why. It was exciting. I liked it. I liked invading their privacy. I looked through all the drawers upstairs, but they were mostly empty. There were some clothes in the closet. I looked through them. I didn't know the people at all, but being in the house gave me the feeling that I did. I liked that. That's why I was sitting in that chair. Just thinking about them, I could almost hear their voices.

"I have this fantasy. I'm in the city, Portland maybe. Whatever. And I see this girl on the street. She's very attractive, so I follow her. I follow her for days, get to know everything she does and everywhere she goes. But she never sees me. I get to know her completely without her ever knowing me. And then when I think I've got her completely down cold, I go away and never come back. Like leaving a lover. She never even knows I was there."

"Voyeurism."

"Sure. I get to be with her, know her, even to care about her a little, but I never have to show anything. I never have to do anything. I'm completely...aloof. At the same time I'm completely committed to her, obsessive even. It's all I do for days. You see?"

"I think so."

We got the car. We sat for a while, letting it idle. And I couldn't get it out of my mind. The whole experience was so clear to me, as though it had only happened days ago. And it was strange, because I could remember *wanting* to get caught in there. That was why the flashlight was on. I'd had it trained right on the window, for no good reason at all except that I must have known somebody would see it and wonder. I'd wanted somebody to know. I think I was even aware of it at the time, without understanding why I'd want to risk that, why I felt that way.

I thought I knew now what the fantasy was about. It was a kind of declaration to myself as to where things stood with me. The reserve. The need for emotional safety. Yet as early as six years ago, I'd broken into a stranger's house and thrown a flashlight beam on the living room window. Even that far back I must have know what my little reserve was worth.

We were quiet going back to Dead River. I didn't take her home. Even at four in the morning it would be quite a scene there. A rock through a window isn't easy to forgive. A rock through a neighbor's window would be nearly impossible to forgive. And Casey wouldn't want forgiveness anyway.

We went to my apartment instead.

We climbed the stairs, yawning. And Casey turned back to me and murmured, "*Sounds like fun*."

"What does?"

I knew what she meant. It made me cold inside. But I went through the motions anyway.

"Breaking and entering."

I said nothing. I opened the door for her. She stepped inside and faced me. The smile was sleepy but the eyes were filled with broken light. I didn't even bother to argue the point. I knew where it would lead us. It was where we'd been going, anyway, all along.

"I want to do it."

The tendrils of fog had followed us from the graveyard. They slid around my throat again like soft wet claws, caressing me, turning my spit to acid.

"And I know just the place for it too. The perfect place."

"You do?"

She looked at me. For the first time, her smile mocked me a little.

"*Don't you*?"

Fourteen

"LOOK, IT *HAS* TO BE THE CROUCH PLACE."

"Why?"

"Because it does."

The hamburgers at Harmon's were lousy. The refrigerated, prepackaged kind you stick in a microwave. But we ate them. Casey looked terrific in a tiny blue halter and cream-colored shorts. The makeup was subtle and carefully done. To me it was obvious there was seduction going on.

"Because the Crouch place is isolated, dummy. I have no intention of getting caught like our cat burglar over here." She nodded at me and Kim smiled.

"Nobody's going to come by. Nobody's going to see us go in or come out again, and nobody's going to pay any unexpected calls. It's perfect."

"She's right," said Steve. "It's the safest place around. But I dunno, Case. Where's the big thrill?"

"It'll be worth it. You'll see."

"Got something planned?" Kim wiped at a crumb of burger bun at the corner of her mouth."

"I might."

"So tell us."

"And make it good, please," said Steve. "Because I really

can't see this so far. I mean, what's the big deal about walking into an empty house at night, looking around and leaving? It's kids' stuff. It would almost make more sense to do it someplace in town. If we *can't* get caught, where's the risk? What's the point?"

"There's no risk. But I can still make it fun. It's kids' stuff, all right. But use your imaginations. You'll see."

"See what?"

"Will you *tell* us for chrissake?"

"Come on, Case," I said. "Let's have it. Skip the buildup."

She looked at me and grinned. I wasn't a conspirator, but I felt like one. Whatever her idea was we hadn't discussed it. She knew damn well I wasn't happy with the thing. I'd go along. She didn't have to sell me like she did the other two. But I wasn't happy.

She was, though.

She'd found a way to shoo the boredom again.

"Hide and seek," she said.

Kim's mouth made a big scowly streak across her face. "*What*?"

Steve looked at her the way an adult will look at an annoying child. I just sat there, thinking about it.

"Hide and seek. Just the way we used to play it when we were kids. But we play it in the Crouch place."

You could feel it dawning on them. It was a dumb idea, all right, but it had possibilities, ambiguities. Personally I'd rather have been in Sheboygan.

"I get it. The place is supposed to be haunted or something, right?" Steve's index finger darted at her like the tongue of a snake.

"Right. So we play with that a little, see? No flashlights allowed. A strange house. At night. Alone. A place we don't know and have never been in before."

Kimberley nodded. "The vague possibility of a cop coming along."

"Very vague," I told her. I hoped I was right.

"But still there," said Casey.

"And us with the lights off, trying to find one another in the dark in an old, weird house." Kim's voice was excited now, the concept in full bloom.

Steve snapped his fingers.

"I like it. I really do. You're right—it's kids' stuff, but it's *good*."

"A whole lot better than *The Love Bug*."

That was the movie at the Colony tonight. Kim shivered.

"I'm spooked already!"

All of them turned to me.

"Dan?" said Casey.

I shrugged. "Why not?"

She leaned over and kissed me on the cheek. It was the kind of kiss you get from grandmothers on your tenth birthday.

"It's settled, then."

She drained her chocolate egg cream. Steve's straw gurgled in the bottom of his glass.

"When do we go?"

"What's wrong with tonight?"

"Sooner the better."

Kim was hopping around in her seat by now. "Okay, so what do we bring?"

"Despite what Casey says, I'd suggest flashlights," I told them. She started to object.

"We don't have to use them, Case. But just to be on the safe side. That house is pretty old, you know. Floors start to go in old houses, things fall down on you. I don't think if one of us got hurt we'd want to depend on matches."

Steve held up the bandaged hand. "He's right."

"I'd also suggest a couple of six-packs. Apart from that, I can't think of anything."

"Time?"

"Midnight, of course," said Kimberley.

Casey nodded. "We should meet—say at Dan's place—at eleven, eleven-thirty."

"Right."

There was a silence then. Everybody smiled at one another. I think we all felt pretty silly. Kim started to giggle.

"You've had some dumb ideas, Casey. But this one..."

"Thanks."

"I mean *really*."

"I appreciate it."

"*Ghosts*, for god's sake!" She threw up her hands. For a moment there was something very Old Testament about it. In Harmon's. A blond girl in shorts. Praying.

There was a lot I had to tell them about the Crouch place, but I waited.

My feeling was that telling them right away would only end in Casey's finding some way around it. A few handy rationalizations here and there and she'd have us going along with no trouble whatsoever.

It seemed my best chance would be to try throwing a scare into them at the last minute and hope somebody balked. I wasn't crazy about *The Love Bug* either, but it was preferable to something that could get me arrested. None of them had ever been caught at anything. I had. I knew it felt lousy. The old stories about Ben and Mary bothered me a whole lot less than the off chance that some nosy local farmer would drive by and realize there was somebody inside there and call the police. I never really credited Rafferty's speculations about strange disappearances, but I credited bad luck. I credited that, all right.

We met at my apartment.

Casey showed up in the same blue halter top and cream shorts, looking like she was ready for a picnic. I told her that if the night turned cold, she was going to freeze out there. She dipped into the green book bag and pulled out the corner of an army shirt, looking at me as if to say, no small objections, thanks. I made no more of them.

Kim wore overalls over a yellow cotton blouse. Both had seen some use. It was a good choice, practical for the kind of thing we were doing. Predictably Steven's shirt was bright with tropical colors—greens, yellows and red-orange—worn over white linen slacks. The swathe of bandage on his hand made him look like an injured tourist in a banana republic. As usual he was last to arrive.

"You're gonna be a mess in that," I told him.

He shrugged. "I'll get clean again."

There were three flashlights between us. Kim had found out hers was broken. I told her she could have mine. It wasn't chivalry. I still wasn't counting on anything happening tonight. I still hoped I could talk them out of it.

We got into the blue Le Baron, and Steven got behind the wheel, and we started off through town.

I waited until we were out on the coast road, with all the houselights and streetlights behind us for maximum effect, and then I spun my little story for them.

I told them about the doctor being afraid and made it sound worse than Rafferty had told it. I told them about the caves and about Ben and Mary being imbeciles who were driven off their land through somebody's greed and made them sound as vengeful as I dared.

Then I wrapped it up.

"Steve, you said there was a light in the house that night. I said bullshit. But suppose you were right? Suppose it's them, in from the caves? Are you folks absolutely sure you'd want to meet up with them in the dark?"

For a while nobody talked, and the atmosphere got pretty strange inside the car. I knew I'd done okay. If I was ever going to turn them back, I'd just taken my best shot, I'd made it weird and spooky. It was so quiet in there you could hear the wind whistle over the hood and the tires thumping over bad road. And there was nobody around for miles. Pretty good place for a ghost story.

It hung in the air a long moment. I could feel the chips stacking up along my side of the table.

For a second or two I thought I had it. Then Casey calmly cut me to ribbons.

"Is that all?"

Her voice was so ordinary-sounding you'd have thought I'd been reciting a shopping list. But at least Steve was a little nervous.

"Jeez, isn't that enough?"

"Of course not. It only makes it better. Dan, I want to ask you something. Do you really believe there's anybody in there?"

"There could be."

"I didn't ask you that. I asked you if you really believed there was. The truth, Dan."

"I'm really not nuts about going in there, Case."

"You're hedging."

I could have lied to her. I could have said, sure, I'm about ninety per cent certain the devil's rolling around in there—but I didn't. I couldn't. We'd both said a lot to each other just the night before. It wasn't a great time to start lying.

"Okay. No, I don't think there is. But I want you to know…there might be."

As limp as wilted lettuce.

Casey smiled. "See? Just as I said. The possibility makes it all the nicer. It was a good try, Dan. Don't worry. If the cops show, we'll cover for you."

"Great."

How she meant to do that I didn't know. Only that she'd read me like a book. And knowing her, I couldn't entirely put it past her. Maybe she had some disappearing act for me in that green bag she was holding in her lap—holding very tightly. I wondered what was in there besides the army shirt. It looked bulky.

I kept kicking myself. Maybe I'd played it badly. Maybe if I'd told them sooner.

We were off to do something dumb again.

Maybe we'd done things just as stupid before but about this one I had a very bad feeling. I could have said forget it, take me home. I could have said I'd wait in the car. I considered both things, then rejected them. It wasn't that I was proving anything, that I was worried about Casey's reaction. I'd have lost a few points. But she'd have gotten over it.

The problem wasn't that. The problem was that without me it would be the three of them alone in there. She'd do it anyway. And the way Kim was giggling beside me again and the way Steve was driving they'd go along no matter what I did. The three of those clowns alone in there.

That thought bothered me.

If anything went wrong I wanted to be inside. I didn't want to depend on Kim and Steve to keep her safe and healthy. Nor did I trust her to take care of herself particularly. She was smart and she was strong, but she took chances. Bad chances. I worried about her.

And there was another thing. Something that now, today, I'm pretty ashamed to admit to.

You see, there was this idiot voice inside me, already creepy-crawling through a dark house in the middle of the night. The voice snickered. It was very cute, very wised-up and cynical.

Besides, it said, *you never know.*

It could be fun.

Fifteen

I KNEW OF A SAFE PLACE TO PUT THE CAR, off a narrow access road through the woods about a quarter of a mile from the house. Nobody would notice it there, at least not till early morning. By then we'd be gone.

Even with the moonlight it was dark. It was one of the few places around where the trees grew tall and spread wide, covering the sky, black pine and birch and poplar. We parked beneath a stand of white birch. When we cut the headlights the trees seemed to carry a glow as though we'd irradiated them with light.

Beyond that it was black.

You could already hear the sea. A distant rumbling. There was no wind. The trees were still. Just the dry scrape of crickets and the faraway tumble and boom of ocean.

"Dan, you know this road, right?"

"Sure, Case."

"Any surprises?"

"Shouldn't be. No big storms this season."

"Then douse the flashlights."

"Why?" There was a tinge of whine to Steven's voice I didn't care for.

"Try it."

I knew what she was after. There we were in the dark, with the smell of damp earth and overheated car around us, listening to the mix of strident arid scrapings and liquid thunder.

"See?"

"Spooky," said Kim.

"That's it."

For a while we just stood and listened, and then Steve said, "I guess that's what we're here for," and the tone of it was more relaxed, and I liked it better. I suppose it's a problem, being rich and spoiled. Even if you grow up pretty decent the only things you have to fall back on are the old, obnoxious habits, and they never make you look like much. In times of stress they come flying back at you like ghosts of squalling children.

We started off down the road, me in the lead, the two girls together behind me and Steve bringing up the rear.

The road was rough and pitted, strewn with rocks and studded with holes, more weathered than I'd thought it would be. If somebody twisted an ankle, it was going to be a very short evening. So I went slowly. For the first couple of yards all you could hear was the four of us scraping along. Then the road got a little better and our walking that much quieter.

It was eerie. Walking in front of everybody, I had the feeling of great aloneness—we four in the empty night. And even we seemed insubstantial. Just sounds of motion like the sea and the rasping of insects. Kim stumbled and cursed and Casey laughed, but aside from that nobody spoke a word. We were made of shoe leather and silence out there, and that was all.

The road got bad again. But the trees broke apart overhead, so you could see a little better. There was a dead branch ahead, and I kicked it out of our way. It made a rustling, crackling sound in the bushes, like a fire burning. Pebbles rolled along with it. On the dry road they were hollow-sounding.

The air was heavy with the scent of evergreen.

Off to the left something moved in the brush. I stopped. The footsteps behind me stopped too. A moment later I saw cattails waving a few feet further on. We'd startled something. A raccoon, maybe. Something roughly that size.

"What was that?" You could hear the thrill in Kim's voice.

"Coon. Possum. Grizzly maybe. It's hard to tell."

There was a moment's pause and then she laughed and called me a bastard.

"Could be a rattlesnake. They grown 'em big around here. So watch your step."

"Could be one of those cockroaches," said Steven. "The big ones. The kind that carry off babies."

"We had them back in Boston," said Kim.

Then they were giggling back there for a while. There was a little tussle going on. I turned around and saw him tickling her. She started squealing. I looked at Casey.

"I don't think we've scared 'em yet. Do you?"

"Just wait."

We turned a bend in the road and then just ahead you could see where the trees stopped and the clearing began, the long grass, weeds and brambles. Framed in the last arch of birch trees you could see the Crouch house, a single black mass against the starry sky.

I'd never approached the house this way at night before. So it was sort of shocking. If ever a house looked haunted, it was the Crouch place. Suddenly all the stories we'd told about it as kids came back to me all at once, and looking at it, you had to wonder if there wasn't a grain of truth in them, as though maybe we'd all had some instinct about the place, some knowledge in the blood and marrow.

How do you credit the creature under the bed? The monster in the closet?

You do but you don't.

It was black, solid black, and because there was nothing but sea behind it, it seemed to drop right off into nowhere. Like the end of something.

The house at the end of the world.

It was bad enough remembering the real things, the things I knew to be true about the place. The dogs. Starved and eaten. The smell of animal waste and bodies bloated with heat and death. The stacks and stacks of newspapers—in a house where nobody could read. The smeared, discolored walls inside.

But there was all the other stuff too. Ideas I'd grown up with, shuddered over, laughed at, scared myself with over and over again. The vampires and the evil and the dead. All that came back too, like a sudden childish vision of madness and cruelty. As we moved through the last stands of trees, as the sky grew bigger overhead, I thought of those things and wondered what I was doing here, like a vulture visiting old corpses.

And I thought about Ben and Mary.

Of idiocy taken to its very extremity. And, in that extremity, made evil.

We broke through to open clearing. Once it had been a pasture. All at once the night sounds seemed to shift and alter around us. Steps were softer. The sea was louder. We were in tall grass now. The crickets screeched us a jibbering welcome.

"Wow," said Kim.

We stopped and looked straight up where she was looking. A huge pool of stars, gouging light into the blue-black sky. The moon was so clear you could see the gray areas against the white.

I've seen a thousand nights like this from a thousand fields, and they never cease to calm me. This one calmed me now.

After a while I said, "Come on."

I've told you I have this habit of staring at the ground ahead of me when I walk. I'd been doing that back on the road, but I wasn't now.

I was focused on that house. Not so nervous now but still focused. Fascinated.

For a while it was nothing but a dark bulk rising off the flatlands, beyond which was nothing you could see. I knew what was back there. A short spit of land and then a cliff dropping down to the sea. I recalled a porch back there and a kind of widow's walk on the second floor.

And then as we got closer you could make out some of the details in front. Gray-brown barn board covering the porch and the entire front of the house, just as it had been in Ben and Mary's time. Three windows on the second floor, shuttered. Two on the first floor, with one of the shutters torn or blown away and an empty pane where the glass should be. Off to the left, an outhouse. A newer wood there—it looked like pine to me. I thought how foul Ben and Mary's must have been, and I guessed the old doctor had replaced it. I would have.

Once there had been a barn. But that had burned down some years ago. I remembered where it was located. The grass grew somewhat longer there.

There were four steps up to the porch. The wood was old, spongy and gave underfoot. So did the porch beams.

The doorway was crude. Strictly post and lintel. It was made of heavy oak, like the door itself. Tacked to the crossbeam of the lintel was a faded blue ribbon, and dangling from the ribbon, facing dead ahead like some bizarre knocker, was a fish-head, mouth agape. The flesh had long since rotted away leaving only three square inches of clean white bone, empty eyed and hollow.

Steve flicked it with his finger. "You put out the welcome mat for us, Case?"

It rattled lightweight against the oak and then was still again. Casey shook her head.

"Nope. Wish I'd though of it. But it's kids, I guess."

"Kids, yeah."

We stood there a moment, feeling awkward, silly. Well, here we were. *Kids*. Casey gave me a grin.

"Who's going to open it?"

I turned the rusted doorknob and gave it a push.

"Locked."

I looked around. I kept having this feeling that somebody had to be watching. We were about to break into a house. So somebody had to know. It was obvious we were going to get caught. I hadn't the luck for anything better.

"There's a window broken over here. One of us can probably slip through and unlock it from the inside."

I looked at Steven.

"Not me." He gestured toward the linen pants. "Whites."

So that was the reason for the beach-party outfit. I took his flashlight from him and walked over to the window. I flicked on the light. I had plenty of room to get through. The window was at chest level. I could hop in easily. But damned if I wanted to.

There was one big spike of glass pointing upward from the bottom pane. I lifted it out of the window and tossed it into the tall grass. There was no sound of breakage.

I turned the beam on the floor inside. There was a lot of broken glass there, but nothing that would get in the way of my climbing in. I swept the bottom pane with the base of the flashlight just to be sure there were no small pieces of glass to grab me. Then I handed it back to Steve.

I turned with my back to the window and reached inside and found the upper line of molding with my fingertips. I brought my head, shoulders and chest inside, and was immediately aware of the cool, moldy smell of the place. Then I pulled myself up and swung my ass and legs into the room. I set myself down in a crunch of broken glass. Steve handed me the flashlight.

Once I was in there the adrenaline really started pumping. That was it. Break-in. From now on they could arrest you.

Shit.

The first thing I did was sweep the room with the flashlight. A brief impression of empty space, an old wooden table and a potbellied stove left behind. I was in the kitchen. It had been a big kitchen. You could see the rust stains on the linoleum floor where the refrigerator had been. There was wallpaper with a fruit-and-berry motif. There were dirty white tiles over the kitchen sink. I thought that at least the moldings over the doors and windows had been scraped and varnished, not painted. The same with the cabinets. Somebody had cared a little.

A two-year-old gas-station calendar hung from a nail on the wall beside me. The month was December. There was a picture of a pair of terrier pups peering over the edge of a Christmas stocking, liquid eyed and plaintive. Directly down the wall from that, over the baseboard, was an empty telephone jack. On the floor lay a small broken end table, over on its side.

I went to the door.

It was double-locked, a Segal lock and a bolt type. I turned the one and threw the other. Casey led them in and I closed the door behind them.

"Lights on," she said, and her beam and Kim's joined mine.

Directly in front of us was the stairwell leading to the second floor, right off the kitchen. The planking looked solid enough. The banisters seemed to have been replaced recently.

I was beginning to realize that I hardly recognized the place. For one thing, I didn't remember any stairwell at all. Maybe there had been too much going on that day. And I'd been pretty young. Maybe the place had done some shape-shifting in my memory since then.

I realized it must have been the kitchen where they'd found the bodies.

Inside, though, the house lost a lot of its ominous quality. Except for Casey, I think we all were glad of that. You couldn't get too worked up over fruit-and-berry wallpaper.

I walked past the stairwell into the living room. Casey followed me. Kim and Steven had a look inside the kitchen.

The living room was pretty empty. A single over-stuffed chair and an old couch with half the stuffing ripped out of them in tiny chunks and scattered all over the floor. I wondered if that was mice. Mice would eat nearly anything, or try to. Then there was another end table, this one still standing, beneath the window to the rear of the house. If you opened the shutters and looked out the window, off to the right you could see the dark weathered boards of the woodshed.

There was a fireplace in the room, and an old set of andirons. A standing lamp and a single straight-back chair made of pine, with one of the dowel spines missing. That was all.

Steve and Kim appeared in the doorway. They leaned into the room and looked around.

"Not many places to hide," said Steve. He turned and deposited a brown bag with two six-packs of beer inside on the kitchen table.

"We'll find places," said Casey. "There's upstairs, and Dan says there's a basement. There's a woodshed right outside this window, if anybody's interested."

Kim made a face. "Yuchh."

"Did anybody find the basement?"

"There's a door off the kitchen." Steve looked slightly embarrassed. "I...we didn't open it."

"That's probably it," I told them. "I didn't notice."

We went into the kitchen. The door was built into the internal wall off to the left opposite the back door to the house, so that the steps ran under the stairwell. I saw why I hadn't noticed it at first. Standing at the window you were blind to it. The door was tiny—only about four-and-a-half feet tall. It looked more like a storage closet.

It was locked.

Casey dug into her book bag. "Try this," she said and handed me a screwdriver.

"You're very resourceful."

"This is news to you?"

The fit between the door and the molding was uneven, so it was easy to slip the screwdriver between them and pry, and I guess the groove was worn away pretty badly, because it gave almost immediately.

"There you go."

"Our hero," said Kim. There was nervous laughter.

The door fell open. Our flashlights played over the old rotten stairs. There was a rough railing constructed of two-by-four pine reinforced with irregular lengths of cheap planking, dark and weathered, as though it had been pulled off some barn and tacked hastily in place. Off to the left you could see the stained, rusted hulk of a boiler.

It was hard to see the rest through the cobwebs.

"I think they're growing 'em big down there," said Steve.

Kim put her hand on Casey's arm. "Do we really have to bother?"

"Of course. It's hideous. Come on."

I offered her the flashlight—Steven had appropriated hers when she'd gone digging for the screwdriver. She gave me an ironic look and took it from me and stepped carefully down the stairs. Halfway down she turned around. The three of us stood there like passengers waiting for a train. I was leaning against the doorframe, a little hunched over, scratching my chin. Kim stood behind me with her arm folded over her chest. Steven was staring at the ceiling, tapping his foot impatiently. We imagined the view from where she stood and broke out laughing.

"You *guys*," she said.

I turned to Kimberley, ignoring her.

"You hear anything?"

"Nah. Nothing but spiders down there."

"I must have heard spiders, then."

"Big, imperious ones."

"I'm giving you five seconds," said Casey, "the three of you, and then I start screaming."

"Coming, Mother," said Kim. "Don't scream."

"Jesus, no," said Steve. "You'll wake the spiders!"

We started down the stairs. Casey held her light for me so I wouldn't go crashing into her. Suddenly, with four pairs of feet on the staircase, things got very noisy.

It's funny how when you're a little scared noise helps.

Maybe you figure that if you announce yourself, the goblins cut and run.

We looked around.

"Gross," said Steven.

It had been a kind of workshop once; you could see that much. Beyond the boiler, against the wall to the far left, was a long, broad wooden table covered with dust and grime, warped and rotting away in places, cluttered with debris from the broken shelves above it. Spilled boxes of nails, broken mason jars that had probably held screws and fittings. A rusted wood plane and a broken rusted hacksaw. The spiderwebs were thick here. I wondered if the doctor had used the place at all.

There was a strange thick smell in the air. I guessed it was mold and mildew, some of it wafting up from a greasy, almost liquid-looking pile of rags off to the far right corner, and some of it from the piles of wood shavings that surrounded the table like gray-yellow anthills. Some of them were near three feet high.

I could also smell paint or varnish, but I couldn't find its source at first. Then Kim brought her flashlight around beneath the table and I could see cans and cans of them, tumbled and spilling all over, their contents freezing them together like some crazy sculpture.

There was another smell too, but I couldn't figure that one.

Kim straightened up. "I take it they weren't big on housekeeping."

"Guess not."

The area toward the back of the house was worse. It looked like the debris of generations there. There was a big grandfather clock, its face broken as though someone had smashed it with a sledgehammer, its works spilling out over the cabinet ledge to the floor. The double cabinets themselves looked dusty but in pretty fair condition. Propped up beside it was an old tin washtub big enough to bathe in, its underside rusted clean away.

Here, too, were all the old accoutrements of farm life. I guessed there hadn't been much lost when the barn burned down. Most everything was in here. A small plow with a broken handle, hoes, rakes, a couple of pitchforks with splayed and broken tines. In one corner a mound of scrap reached halfway up the wall—shovels, an old harness, horseshoes, buckets filled with nails and keys and doorknobs, a curry-comb, locks, window fittings, a dog's studded collar, pots and pans, a gunstock, rimless wheels, a pair of flatirons, a whip, buckles, belts, work gloves, knives, a dull pitted axe. We stood back and looked. You didn't want to get too close to it at all.

"This place is crawling with antiques," said Kim.

"Junk," said Steve.

"No, there are some good things here. Funny nobody's gone through the stuff."

"Probably the stink drove 'em out."

He was right about that. The smell was much worse over here.

"It's driven me out, anyway."

He headed for the stairs. I followed him. I'd seen enough. We got to the top and went to the window and filled our lungs with clean night air.

The cellar would be a good place to hide, I thought, if you could stand it long enough. I wasn't sure I'd want to. Maybe there would be something better—and cleaner—on the second floor.

Kim and Casey followed us up. Kim brushed nervously at the cobwebs on her shirt. Casey looked happy as a clam.

"Well, that much has character, anyway."

Steven looked at her sourly. "What it has is stink."

"Let's try the second floor."

"Nuts," I said.

"What's that."

"I wanted to look for that plaster job I told you about. In the wall. Forgot all about it."

"You can look later. Let's see the upstairs first."

Once there had been pictures hanging along the stairwell. You could see the brighter areas marking their placement on the cream-colored walls, empty windows to nothing.

At the top of the stairs, a few paces down the hall, there was a square trapdoor in the ceiling. I pointed it out to them.

"Attic. It'll be hard to reach."

"I'm not going up there," said Kim.

Casey thought about it.

"We'd need a chair or something."

There was a straight-back in the living room that would do, but I didn't remind her of it.

"Okay. The attic's out of bounds, then."

"Fine."

We walked the short narrow corridor to the front of the house. Kim opened the door on the right-hand side.

"It's a bedroom."

We went in. There was an old stained box spring on the floor and a cheap wood frame stacked in pieces neatly behind it. A ceramic table lamp, its shade missing, stood next to it in front of the window. The room was long, running the entire length of the house. The master bedroom. Steve pulled open the closet door.

A mouse scuttled around in confusion and disappeared through a hole in the baseboard.

There was nothing else inside but a dozen wire hangers and a rolled-up bolt of wallpaper, the same ugly stuff that papered the kitchen.

I glanced out the window, wondering if you could see where we'd parked the car from here. You couldn't. In the moonlight the overgrown field was gray and the trees were a solid craggy wall of black. You couldn't have found a tank back there.

It gave me a funny feeling.

Like we were cut off somehow.

There was another window to the rear of the house and a door, and I knew that behind the door was where the widow's walk would be. But I didn't have a chance to look for it. Casey was in a hurry. She and Kim had already moved into the room opposite this one. I followed them.

Another bedroom, but smaller.

In this one the bed was standing, in a knock-kneed sort of way. You wouldn't have wanted to sit on it, though, even if it hadn't been completely filthy. There was a deep impression in the center, as though whoever had slept here was a pretty good size. We bent down and looked underneath. A lot of the springs were missing. There was nothing underneath but huge balls of dust, so thick you could hardly see the floorboards.

There was a thin faded throw rug bunched up in one corner. A night table with a built-in mirror and a chair. The mirror was broken, but there was no trace of the glass. Otherwise the table looked salvageable, if you cleaned it up considerably. An empty picture frame lay facedown on the table, a comb and a brush and two old nylon stockings moldering beside it.

We opened the drawers. Empty.

Steven pointed to the stockings. "Hers," he muttered.

He opened the closet. There were more wire hangers.

"No mouse."

We walked down the hall past the stairwell to the back of the house. There was a door dead ahead and one to the right.

To the right was yet another bedroom, completely empty. No bed, no mattress. Not even a telltale item of junk on the floor or in the closet.

It was the other door that interested me. The widow's walk.

While the others checked the closet I went out into the hall, found that the door was open, and walked outside.

They weren't far behind me, but there was a moment at least when I was out there alone, breathing the tangy sea air, which was so good after the closed-up, musty smell of the place. The view was really fine. Only a couple of yards from where I stood the property ended in a spectacular drop to the sea. Between the drop and the elevation of the house, you got the feeling of immense height. Far below was the moonlit sea, a shifting mask of darks and lights. There was no wind, but there was still the impression of movement underfoot—the sea. You felt as though you were standing aboard a huge tall raft, just drifting there, alone.

"Pretty good."

Steven moved through the door behind me. Kim and Casey were behind him. There was something about it that made you want to whisper.

"Gee," said Kim. "I can see why they'd fight for the place."

I shook my head. "It wasn't this. It was the house, the land. Their home. And they didn't fight, did they? They just resisted thinking about it, probably, until they couldn't manage that anymore. Then they left.

"I don't know. Can an idiot enjoy something like this? I'm not sure they can."

"Ask Casey," said Steven.

She ignored him. We stood silently for a while, and the raft feeling continued for me. Stars and sea and drift. I began to feel a little dizzy.

"I'm going back inside."

Casey nodded. "Time we all did."

We walked back through the hall and she led the way downstairs. At the foot of the stairs she stopped and turned and told us to have a seat.

Steve and Kim sat on the third step together with me perched two steps above them. Casey turned off her flashlight, and Steve and Kim followed her lead. We sat in the dark.

For the first time the heavy silence of the house settled around us. In the darkness you tended to forget how ordinary it was inside and how empty. The dark had its own fullness. You started remembering all the dumb stories again and seeing the place as you had coming through the forest—not a very normal little house at all, but something grimmer, fatal, with its cruel history.

"*In my bag,*" said Casey, "*I have lengths of nylon rope*."

We waited for her to continue. Her voice had a somber edge to it, commanding and disquieting. I looked for Steve and Kim just two steps away from me and couldn't make them out.

I sighed. The spook show had begun.

Sixteen

"HIDE AND SEEK, THAT'S THE GAME. I've thought up some rules. See if you agree."

"I've got four lengths of rope. One of them is short. We'll draw, and whoever gets the short one will be *it*."

It. I've rarely heard a word sound so silly. Even Casey had to smile.

"That's right, laugh. In this house that might not be as foolish as it sounds. Am I right?"

We stopped laughing. One for Casey.

"Okay, then. Whoever's it will count to one hundred, then come after us. The starting point might just as well be here. The idea is to find us in the dark. No flashlights to be used at any time. All right so far?

"Now. When we used to play this as kids, the first one to be found was it again, and the whole thing started over. But that way it could go on forever. I'm assuming we don't want to bother with that. Nobody intends to spend the whole night here, right? On the other hand, with a little good luck, one of us could get found in two minutes, which doesn't make for much of a game. So I thought of a compromise.

"Whoever's it will take the ropes along. As soon as he or she finds someone, he'll tie that person up as securely as possible and then come looking for the others. When he or she finds the second person, same thing. Bind 'em and then go looking for the third.

"So that the game only ends when everybody's found. That way there's only one round. And two people have the good or bad luck—depending on your point of view—to be tied up hand and foot in an old dark house, waiting for the game to end.

"How does that sound?"

Nobody responded for a minute or two. We just looked at her.

Steven looked astonished.

"*Ropes*? Why not chains, handcuffs? What is this, *The Story of O*? Till Eulenspiegel? I didn't know you were into kinky shit, Case. I thought you were just nuts."

"Can you think of a better way to make somebody stay put?"

"I can think of a better way to spend a Saturday night, if you really want to know the truth."

"The car's waiting."

"Aw, Jesus, Case. Come on."

Personally I had to give it to her. You know the saying about somebody's walking over my grave? Well, I had whole troops marching over mine, making the hackles rise. You could imagine it so easily, that sense of helplessness in the dark. Waiting, while the old house creaked and trembled. Still kids' stuff but with an added fillip of tension. That extra risk she'd promised us.

"I *like* it," said Kim.

"I think you're both very sick," said Steve.

"You playing or aren't you?"

"*Listen* to yourself, Case! 'You playing or aren't you?' What are we, twelve?"

"What's bothering you, Steven? Kink or dignity. Or maybe you're just scared."

"Shit." He thought about it, though. In a minute he started to smile. We all did. "*Dignity*," he said. "Okay, let 'er rip. Let's have your lengths of rope, dear."

"For this we'll need a light."

She flicked hers on. She drew four rope ends out of the

green book bag. Nylon climbers' rope. Thin, pliant and very sturdy.

I asked her, "How short's the short one?"

She grinned. "You'll know it when you see it. Patience."

Kim was looking at her. "You think you've been pretty cute about all this, doncha."

Haven't I?"

"I dated an egomaniac once. We'd go to bed together. I knew he was an egomaniac, see, because when he was coming, he'd scream his own name."

"Very funny."

"I think I need a beer," said Steven.

"Later."

"How much later?"

"After you draw."

"In that case I'll go first."

He tugged one up out of the bag. It was four feet long. He smiled.

"Can I have that beer now?"

"Yes."

She was very intent, playing it to the hilt and enjoying every moment.

"Four-foot lengths?" I asked her.

She nodded.

"Two for each person. Four of them total, since only two of us will need to get tied. The other one's in the bottom of the bag here."

"That should do it."

"I'd hope so. You ready, Kim?"

Kim had her right hand over her left breast, cupping it in pure unconscious anxiety. She realized what she was doing and the hand fluttered away. I caught her glance. It was shy and full of pleasure, like a kid caught with her hand in the cookie jar. I nodded toward the bag.

"You first."

She closed her eyes and reached for it. The line came up long. That left Casey and me.

Steve came back into the room with beers for all of us. Kim chugged hers greedily.

"I'm going to need another of these before we get started."

Steven belched. "Just remember there's no indoor plumbing. You'll have to use the outhouse."

"Thanks, I'll use the lawn."

"Once we start, the woods and the lawn will be out of bounds, okay?" said Casey.

"Sure."

She refused the beer Steve offered her. I took mine and popped the tab. She was staring at me. I knew what she wanted. "Okay, okay," I told her.

I reached into the bag.

The first tug told me it was too light. I pulled it out all the way. About one foot long. I let it dangle. Casey reached for the last one. Four feet, like the others.

"Dan's it."

I made myself look glum. "Sure. Screw the local kid."

"I'll take that beer now," said Casey.

Steve handed it to her and she shook it and then popped the tab. Suds went flying all across the hall. Plenty of it landed on Kim's yellow blouse just above the line of overalls.

"Shit! What do you want him to do, *smell* me out?"

"Sorry."

"Jeez, Case!"

"You get good ideas, and you get bad ones. Sorry."

She wasn't really angry, though. We sat quietly sipping our drinks. Kim finished hers quickly and went to the kitchen for another. She returned and said, "Hey, lights out. Remember the rules, huh?"

Steven didn't like it. "We can't even finish our beers?"

"Ask the referee."

Casey turned off her flashlight.

"Getting into this, huh, Kim?"

"A little."

"One problem," I said. "You haven't given me the ropes yet."

"And I haven't finished my damn beer."

"Okay," said Casey. "Lights on again."

She set her flashlight down on the floor with the beam running across it into the kitchen and dug into the book bag. She pulled out another four-foot length of rope. Steve handed me his and Kim gave me hers. I looped them all together and loosened my belt a couple of notches and pushed them through the belt in front so they wouldn't get snagged in the dark.

"Who gets the flashlights?"

Casey thought about it. "I guess we can leave them here on the table with the beer and stuff. That's the best way to make sure nobody cheats and uses one."

"You take 'em," said Kim. "Put them in the book bag. We trust you. I might be tempted to steal one."

"I'm not sure *I* trust me."

Steven shrugged. "It's your game, Case. You willing to cheat yourself?"

"I guess not."

"Then take them. I finished my beer, by the way."

"Lights out, then." They were all ready to go. I could have used another drink.

Casey turned the world dark again.

I felt her hand thrust its fingers between mine, twining them, exerting a gentle pressure. Her body shifted next to me, and I put my arm around her waist. She turned and there we were for a moment, necking in the dark.

The first kiss was warm and sweet, the second more playful. She nipped at my bottom lip and I could feel her own lips turn up into a smile.

"Good luck."

"Good luck to you, sport."

"You really think it's crazy?"

"No more than usual."

"I like you, Dan Thomas. Even if you do have two first names."

"Fond of you too, Case."

Kim whispered, "You ready?"

I took a deep breath, inhaling Casey's scent as she moved away from me.

For a moment the three of them shifted in a pack, a human shell game. There were ropes dangling against my leg. It was batty. I closed my eyes.

"Ready."

I started counting.

I listened to the footsteps clatter on the hardwood floor. Someone went upstairs. Maybe two people did, or one person moving double-time to confuse me. I couldn't be sure. Somebody moved softly into the kitchen. And I remembered from childhood how hard it was to follow the sound of footfalls through the drone of your own voice counting, echoing inside you.

Twenty-nine. Thirty.

All at once I had the maddening urge to giggle. I resisted it.

Forty. Forty-one.

I felt a tightening in my bladder that wasn't entirely the beer.

Upstairs I heard shifting, scraping.

I remembered the softness of the kiss, the playful biting.

I kept counting.

Seventeen

THE DARKNESS WENT MOLECULAR ON ME, filled with spots of light.

I squinted my eyes shut. They wanted to open. My face

muscles wouldn't let them. A dim widening amber color began to burn at the core of my vision.

I was a whole lot better at this, I thought, as a kid.

I was leaning on the windowpane, dizzy as a fresh-water sailor.

"Ninety-eight. Ninety-nine. One hundred."

I opened my eyes.

I was wildly out of focus, blinking out toward the high grass and trees. And then I did focus.

Out there in the grass, something blinked back at me.

I jumped.

It was as though I'd been leaning on a hotplate. Neck, arms, back and shoulders jerked back involuntarily. My arms slammed shut like traps. My mouth made a little wet popping sound as the jaw dropped open.

It was unexpected as a cobra in the upstairs bathroom. The brain takes a clout from the nervous system. And it's a moment before you start working again, before the gears mesh, and you can see what you saw.

I looked again.

Two eyes, not twenty feet away. Unmistakable. Shifting and glowing in the moonlight.

I saw them clearly for a moment, and then they dropped away, lower into the dense grass, and disappeared. I kept watching. Seconds later I saw a line of movement through the grass and followed it for about ten feet or so before that disappeared too. It was moving in the direction of the trees. Roughly, toward the car.

Whatever it was, I knew it wasn't human. The eyes had been too small and spaced too closely together.

So what was it, then? Raccoon? Possum?

Dog?

Please, *no dogs*, I thought.

A pussycat would be nice.

It was gone, though. And I had this damn fool game to play.

I decided tentatively on raccoon. Then I realized I'd forgotten something.

"Coming!" I yelled. "Here I come."

I omitted the traditional "ready or not." You could only go so far.

I reviewed what little I'd heard. One or maybe two of them were upstairs. One had gone into the kitchen. Off the kitchen there was a back door and the door to the cellar, so whoever had gone that way could have used either one of them. I did not relish exploring either the cellar or the woodshed without benefit of flashlight, so I hoped whoever had gone that way would feel the same. If it was Casey, I was probably in trouble. But I decided to leave that possibility for last.

I went upstairs.

I had to go slowly. Halfway up it got very dark, then brighter as I approached the landing. There was a window in the door leading out to the widow's walk, and a beam of moonlight shining through. It was the only illumination.

Where to hide?

I knew where I'd go.

I'd take the widow's walk.

Not because it was a particularly good place to hide—it wasn't—but because it was nice out there. The most accommodating place the house had to offer. So, if I wasn't too heavily into the game in the first place, at least I'd have a good easy spot to sit it out.

I wondered if any of the others would think that way.

Sure. Steven would.

He was sitting just outside the door, sipping a beer. He glanced at me and smiled.

"Have some?"

I squatted down beside him. "Don't mind if I do."

"Nice and easy, right?"

"Very easy." I tasted the beer. It was half-empty.

"Good."

"I didn't think you were into this much."

"Well, the idea's better in principle than it is in execution. Who wants to spend half an hour under a dusty old bed or something?"

"Casey might."

He snorted. "Casey would."

He looked up at the sky. "This is not bad, though."

"Not at all." I handed him back the beer. "I'm supposed to tie you up."

"Yeah."

"It feels...pretty dumb."

"Of course it does. How did you think it was going to feel? Hell, Dan, you're all grown-up now."

"Yeah."

"You'd better do it, though." He sighed. "Who knows. Maybe the girls are really getting a kick out of this. Maybe they *like* dust." He looked up at the sky again. "It shouldn't be too bad out here."

"No."

"Or too nervous-making." He slugged down the rest of the beer and glanced back over his shoulder. "Everything's strange back down that way."

There was no point in telling him what I'd seen on the lawn. No sense worrying the guy. No animal was going to bother him out here unless it sprouted wings.

I took two of the nylon cords off my belt and he pressed his wrists together obligingly. I ran two loops around them and two between them and knotted it off. Then I tied his feet together just above the ankles. If he wanted to, I guessed he'd be able to untie his legs easily enough. I didn't care. With a little luck it would be over soon anyhow.

"Not too tight, is it?'

"No, it's fine. Do me a favor, though?"

"What's that."

"Play this smart, Dan. If you find everybody as fast as you found me it's going to be over in five minutes—and you know Casey. She'll want another round. So if it looks that easy, play it a little stupid, will you?" I nodded. "I'll give you a hint, though. Kim's up here somewhere."

"Any idea where?"

"Not really. I just heard her follow me up the stirs. I think she got rid of her shoes on the landing, because then I couldn't hear her anymore."

"Thanks."

"Don't mention it. And I mean that literally. Kim would kill me."

"Don't worry."

"Casey too."

"Jesus, Steve."

"Okay, okay."

I walked out and closed the door behind me. First I tried the empty room, though I didn't think that very likely. Steve would have heard her if she'd come that far. Besides, there was nowhere to go but the closet.

I was right. It was empty.

I walked down the hall, my footsteps sounding very big to me. For once my habits paid off. I was staring down ahead of me. And there were her sneakers right by the landing, off to one side. I'd walked right by them before while my eyes were adjusting to the light. I picked them up. So she was barefoot now.

I heard two sets of sounds just then. One set came from below, from the first floor or the cellar. A voice. And then something metallic, like something falling. Casey. Probably stumbling over something or other.

The other sound was nearer. A scuffling in the master bedroom. It could have been Kim, and then again it could have been mice. I opened the door quietly and looked inside.

Something was different.

I couldn't figure what at first, but something. I listened. The sounds had stopped.

With windows to the front and back the light was pretty good here. I walked in. I still couldn't figure what it was that bothered me about the room. I walked over to the box spring and looked behind the frame, even though you couldn't have hidden a bag of groceries back there. I was looking for what bothered me.

Then I saw it. The ceramic table lamp, sitting on the floor. It had a shade now. Some droopy kind of thing. There had been no shade before. I plucked at it.

Kim's beer-stained blouse.

I think I smelled it before I recognized it. I lifted it off the works. Very cute, Kim, I thought. I bet you look just dandy in your overalls.

I walked to the closet and opened the door, fully expecting to see her crouching there. There was a scuttling in the darkness near the floorboards. Just the mouse again, only this time he'd brought a friend. They froze, waiting for me to do something.

I did.

I took Kim's overalls off the wire hanger.

I couldn't help laughing. Somewhere there was a naked woman running around in socks and panties. Leaving me a trail to follow. It seemed that Kim was making up her own game.

Meantime I was piling up quite a wardrobe.

I shut the door and left the mice to whatever they were up to in there, and walked out into the hall. There was only one room left, so that had to be it. If Steven was right about her being upstairs, this was where I'd find her.

A pair of socks were draped over the inside doorknob. I added them to my collection.

"Okay, Kim," I said.

I listened. Heard nothing.

There were a number of options. The closet, obviously. Under or behind the night table. Under the bed. Under the bunched up throw rug.

The rug looked just as it did before. I lifted it anyway and was glad I did.

In the moonlight Kim's panties looked to be a very light shade of blue.

I listened again. The room was silent. I walked to the closet and flung open the door. Wire hangers rattled at me like budget wind chimes.

I closed it again. I got on my hands and knees and peered under the bed. That was empty too, except for thick gray waves of dust. There was nobody under the dresser and no way to fit in behind it. So where the hell was she?

There was nothing left in the room.

Steven's either wrong or she got by me, I thought. Damn.

I heard a rattling sound behind me. The distance was odd. It sounded muted, like it was here in the room with me but *not* here, exactly. A shadow fell across me. I whirled around.

It was the second time I'd jumped tonight. And much worse than the first one. Much worse.

She was framed in the corner of the window from the waist up, at an angle, right shoulder low and right arm dangling limp at her side. She seemed to sway, brushed by the wind. Her head lolled off to the right, thrown slightly back. Her mouth was open and eyes stared blankly into the room.

The stocking cut deep into the flesh of her neck. It ran taut behind her head to some point out of sight.

I felt a jolt inside me that was somewhere between adrenaline and heart attack. Then suddenly I was at the window, flinging it up and open.

I reached for her, touched cool flesh.

She smiled.

"Gotcha," she said.

I looked down. She was standing on top of the woodshed. On tiptoe. The end of the stocking was in her left hand. Both the outstretched arm and the end of the stocking had been out of my line of vision. She laughed and let the stocking fall, twirled it like a scarf, bumped at me like a stripper.

I could easily have wrung her neck.

I settled for verbal abuse. It got pretty creative. All she did was laugh. It was slightly hysterical sounding. I think she'd half scared herself out there—it was that kind of laughter. Finally I ran out of things to call her so I helped her back inside.

"I ought to leave you out there, you know that?"

"Poor Dan."

"I ought to tie you up and leave you there."

"You wouldn't do that. It's *chilly*."

I looked at her breasts. The nipples were tightly puckered. "I can see that. I suppose you'll want your clothes back too."

"Please?"

"Why not."

I handed them over. All except the panties. "These I'm keeping as a souvenir."

"Whatever turns you on, hon."

I watched her dress. In the moonlight it was an extremely pretty body.

"You scared the shit out of me," I told her. By now, though, I could say it calmly.

"Sorry."

"Sorry my ass. You loved it."

"I did."

"How do you feel about bondage?"

"I *love* bondage!"

She finished buttoning her blouse.

I told her to sit on the floor and put her hands behind her back. I tied them together with one of the ropes, not too tightly, but enough so that she wouldn't be working them free in a hurry. I wanted this one to stay put, exactly where I placed her. Not like Steven. I wanted her to pay a little. I bound her feet. Then I picked her up under the armpits and dragged her to the closet.

"Hey! Where we going?"

"You'll like it here. Nice and spooky."

I opened the door. Then I lifted her again and started moving her inside. She gave me some trouble.

"Hey! Come on! Not in there. It's gonna be dark in there!"
"Sure is."
"Come on, Danny, please?"
"Sorry, sweets."
There was just enough room for her to stretch out a little. Standing up was going to be tricky, though. Even if she did, she'd find that the door locked from the outside.
"Danny! Daannny*yyyy*!"
I closed the door and threw the lock.
"Don't worry," I told her. "The mice are in the other closet, remember? At least I think they are. Bye now."
I walked away. She could curse pretty well herself. I heard her practicing all the way down the stairs.

Eighteen

IT WAS FUN AT FIRST.
Where's Casey? Casey in the kitchen?
Nope.
Casey in the living room?
Unh-unh. Casey in the shed?
Then it stopped being fun abruptly.
Casey in the basement.
Oh, shit.
There was a little light on the cellar stairs filtering down from the first-floor windows, but you can imagine how far that got me. Not even off the stairs. And from there on it was a dark such as I'd never experienced before and hope never to experience again. I could almost feel my pupils widening, struggling to accommodate to the idea that this was a whole new ball game for human eyesight.
For a while all I could do was stand and wait. It was wait or grope and I didn't feel like groping. Leave it to Casey, I thought. Down here it *was* scary. Not like traipsing through the bedrooms.

Down here you could fall on your ass and die on the flat of an axe or the tines of a pitchfork. It made me worry a little about that sound I'd heard earlier.

I must have waited five minutes on the stairs. It never got much better than a dull gray, filled with shapes of solid black. I was glad we'd explored earlier, otherwise I'd never have known that heap of debris was just that or been able to recognize the huge frozen man-shape of the boiler for a boiler. I'd have turned and ran.

It was bad enough to take a step forward and feel spider-webs along your face and neck. Bad enough to kick something rag soft and feel it curl around your foot like the tiny fingers of a child. Bad enough to smell the smells down there. You didn't need big amorphous shapes to unhinge you any further. But there they were anyway.

And I thought all the while I was upstairs, she's been down here.

Not me, brother.

No way. You are crazy, Case. A crazy case. Rafferty was right. More guts than brains. Infinitely more.

So get into it, I thought. If she can, so can you. Get a little crazy. Laugh. Giggle a little, like Kim. Kim locked away in the closet. Wish I hadn't done that. Sort of cruel. Like this is cruel. Get into it, will you? Play bogeyman.

"I'm coming to *get* you, Casey."

Voice like a dying owl. More scared than scary.

"Where are you-oooo?"

No sound. Just smells. The smell of something rotten. I thought of the mice upstairs. Dead mouse somewhere. I stepped slowly, groping. Didn't want to grope. Had to. Hands groping, feet groping too inside the shoes. Small easy steps to the work-table. Past the boiler (see? it's just a boiler). No Casey behind it. Piles of sawdust ahead of me like giant anthills. Feel around for the worktable. Greasy-feeling. Old sour wood. Used too long, too long between usages. Peer underneath, eyes open wide, full throttle. Just paint cans. No Casey.

I kicked over a box of nails, heard them rattle across the floor. Good work, I thought. Makes walking more treacherous than it already is. Great. A genius at spelunking, every step a masterpiece. I moved to the right.

A pile of something in the right-hand corner. Can't remember what it is, sure as hell can't see. Small steps toward it, hands held out in front of me, waving a little. Like Frankenstein's monster, just learning how to walk. I could feel something slippery underfoot, a grease spot or something.

Rags. A pile of old dirty rags. Even Casey wouldn't hide in there. The other side of the room, then. Toward the back of the house.

A faint breeze coming from that direction. The smell of rot moving along with it.

I shuffled past the stairway and tried to see inside it through the stilts and crossbeams. It was way too dark.

"Casey?"

No answer. Maybe you had to say gotcha. Damn stupid game.

"Gotcha!"

Shit.

Then suddenly I had it. I knew where she was. I was sure of it.

The grandfather clock.

I'd noticed the first time we were down that the clock was the cabinet type. You could hide in there. And if I'd noticed it, then you could bet that so did Casey. I thought it would be just like her to find the only item in the house that could remotely be called elegant and use that for a hideout. She was nuts but she had class. It was the clock, all right.

Now if I could only find the damn thing.

If anything, it was even blacker here. The dim beam of light from upstairs played out completely. It couldn't turn the corners, couldn't slip through the stairs and crossbeams, wasted itself on cans of paint and piles of rags and looming hulks of whatnot.

Where are you when I need you, moon? You could hardly tell where the wall began at first. It was just black. My dilated pupils expanded one last time and then gave up, rolled over in mute surrender.

I proceeded like a blind man. Used my other senses. *Touch*. (Cobwebs.) *Smell*. (Dampness, rot.) *Hearing*. (Somebody in here needs walking lessons.)

"Casey? Out of the clock, Casey."

Silence. I guessed she was going to make me work for it.

Something crawled across my face, and I almost lost it right then and there. I'm pretty sure I screamed. I know I batted at my face until my jaw hurt and I felt something wet and cool smear across my cheek.

I hate spiders. Spiders and snakes.

Spiders and snakes and the dark.

Casey'd pitched me two out of three.

There was a great urge to say fuck this and light a match. I crushed it between gritted teeth.

When I stopped trembling, I moved on.

I was trying to remember whether the clock was to the left or to the right, but I couldn't. There had been too much junk there. It numbed the mind. I'd have to do it slowly, by feel mostly. Finally I reached the wall. In front of me was a small plow—at least I thought it was a plow. I felt like one of the old blind men with the elephant in that proverb. ("*This here's an anaconda*.") But I was pretty sure I had it right.

As I moved to the left, my foot scraped a bucket of some kind. I reached down into it and felt a dusty old belt buckle. There were other pails too. Nails, window fittings. I was beginning to remember. If I'd been able to muster the patience, I knew my eyes would eventually adjust even to this level of darkness. But that spider had unnerved me.

Memory told me the clock was in this direction. The whole big mound of stuff was to my right. So the clock was left. I kept going.

I leaned toward the wall and felt it with the palms of my hands. The tines of a garden rake. Beside it, a shovel. I scraped along slowly. There was a tenpenny masonry nail in the cement and, dangling from it, a big brass key. Something that felt like a birdcage beside it. Horseshoes. Another shovel. A whip. The wall felt cold, rough and slimy.

The breeze was stronger here.

I kicked something hard and metallic, felt it slide away a little. I edged toward it and bent down.

The washtub.

I remembered the washtub. It had been propped up right beside the clock. Now it was down, resting on its base. But that meant the clock was...

Right here.

I could even see its outlines now. I reached for it.

The cabinet doors were open.

Inside, it was empty.

Something sour started happening in my stomach, and it wanted out of me. There was too much darkness. It was making me dizzy, the way you feel after a night with too much beer and nothing to eat when you lie down in bed and close your eyes and everything starts to move on you, swirling, rolling like film badly sprocketed in a projector. I couldn't understand it. Where was she? Incomprehension buckled half my brain, and what was left was instinct, and instinct told me the appropriate emotion was fear. I needed badly to sit down, to stop the sudden sweating, the cold sweats that had come on with the urge to vomit. Because if she was not here.

She was nowhere.

Not possible.

There was a trick somewhere. Had to be. Remember Kim at the window?

Something fishy. Hoaxing the local kid.

Not nice, Casey. Cut it out. I will wet my drawers if you don't.

"Casey! Goddamn you, Casey! Get the fuck out here, right NOW!"

You are roaring, son. Like a lunatic. And not a thing has come of it. Nobody home. No results to your inquiry. Inefficacy. Failure.

"Please!"

You are whistling, so to speak, in the dark.

That part of my mind that was still working told me to get the others, fast, that this was not for me alone anymore and no game. So I turned for the stairs. And forgot the clutter.

I don't know what tripped me. A rake, maybe, a hoe—something with a long wooden handle. But I went down like a sack of flour, flat down on my chest, stomach and thighs, feet flying out behind me. I heard two sounds simultaneously: the thunk of my forehead against concrete and the woosh of air out of my lungs. Then a moment of pain and a slow struggle with unconsciousness. At first strictly touch and go. Out of one blackness into another. I fought it. It cost me a massive effort of will just to sit up, another to check for damages.

There was a wet spot on my forehead high up near the hairline, chilly in the cold draft across the floor. And that was all. I figured I'd gotten off easy.

I was aware of a strong, fetid odor. The smell of old meat spoiling.

I'd smelled it before but it was much stronger now, infecting the cool summer breeze. I thought of death. I thought of a stale shallow tide pool of seawater and rotted bivalves. I thought of skeletons scattered throughout the litter of pots, pans, pitchforks and knives around me. Not the skeletons of mice, either. I saw Ben and Mary crawling out from under. The skeletons of cannibalized dogs.

The floor was wet, slick to the touch. I pushed myself up. I reached into my pocket for a match. The game was over. I lit one and held it in front of me. I cupped the match in my hands and stared into the breeze. I thought of what Rafferty had told me about long ago, a quiet warning none of us had heeded.

I moved along on hands and knees. There was no sound but my own scraping sounds and the relentless gentle wind breathing at me. I crawled in the dark. No more falling. In the match light I had seen it well enough—a rough circular hole broken through the wall, no more than two or three feet in diameter. Room to crawl through, or out of, but no more. I followed the current of air, the damp scent of it, slowly.

I approached it like the doorway to hell.

I knew she'd gone inside.

The smell wouldn't bother her, not for the short duration it would take for me to find her. The darkness, the smell, the fear—all that would make it more attractive. You fool, I thought. You damned idiot.

Make me mistaken.

I lit a match. I examined the opening. It was a tunnel cut or scraped through the foundation. The clock was angled in such a way that, standing, that and a pile of newspapers hid it partially from view. Lying to one side was the old metal bucket. Was that what Casey had tripped over—the sound I'd heard upstairs? I pushed away the papers and leaned inside.

I looked more closely. I saw broken concrete heaped to one side. As though the hole had been dug from *inside* the tunnel.

Beyond the foundation work the tunnel led back a few feet through solid rock and then turned a corner, so that the rest of it was blind, its depth unknowable.

I didn't want to go in there.

I seemed to know two things about it instinctively. There was something dead in there and something else alive. I could smell the death. Whoever or whatever was alive, it wasn't just Casey. I don't know how I knew that, but I did.

The match went out. I lit another, cupping it against the breeze.

"Case?"

Holding the match in front of me, I took a deep breath and held it in my lungs and worked my way carefully into the hole.

It died before I'd gone two feet. I lit three of them together and got almost to the corner before they died too. The wind was stronger now. In the dark it seemed thicker, seawater damp. The rocks above and below me breathed moisture. My throat was bone-dry.

I lit up the rest of the pack and lurched ahead, holding the matches like a torch in front of me, and rounded the corner. It illuminated only three feet or so of what appeared to be a long tunnel, utterly black beyond the glow. But it was enough. Enough to see.

The green book bag lay almost beneath my hand.

I reached for it, gripping the tough cloth, something clean and fresh in that foul place, and dragged it toward me. I heard a rattle of lightweight metal. I reached inside. Two of the flashlights were still there.

I pulled one out and turned it on and threw its beam down the tunnel.

Like a child I wanted very much to cry.

The third flashlight lay five feet away from me, abandoned.

Beyond it I could see nothing but emptiness and sweating gleaming rock. Twenty feet on there was another blind turn. I listened.

There was something alive out there.

Something alive on the wind beyond my beam of light.

I listened to it. And I knew it was listening to me.

It wasn't that there was any sound, just a presence. But a powerful one. Something that told me I dared not call out to her again, dared not move forward or even back. I froze. Whatever it was, it would be happy to kill me. I knew that. I knew it on some basic animal level where we all are hunters and hunted, where there are still savannas and jungle moonlight. It was there, just around the corner. An intelligence that was not the same as mine. Measuring me.

I did something purely instinctive. I think it saved my life. I doused the light.

And waited. The smell of death in the air, mine or Casey's or perhaps its own. I would meet it in a matter of seconds now, and then one of us would see.

I waited. And for a long time I didn't move at all. I tried to breathe evenly, quietly, calmly. And still I felt it measuring me, testing the air for the shrill scent of fear in me. I tried to shepherd the fear back to some deep place inside where calm could protect and shield me and maybe breed an uncertainty of its own. Moments passed.

While I waited, Casey could be dying.

There was no choice. I knew what I knew.

I heard it breathing. Shallow, moist and heavy. As though through clotted blood.

It was possible to imagine anything in there.

In the dark.

For a long while I was only a heartbeat. Then I sensed a change.

I waited to be sure.

Whatever it was, it was gone.

I didn't even bother turning on the light. I backed out the way I'd come. Fast.

With the flashlight in one hand and her book bag in the other, I ran for the stairs. I sprinted them two at a time.

I remember only silence from this. Not the sounds of my own footsteps nor the sounds of my own heavy breathing. Only silence. My own strange motion through the hall and up the second flight of stairs.

Down the corridor to Steven.

Nineteen

I THINK HE MUST HAVE TAKEN ONE LOOK AT ME and known everything.

"What's wrong?"

With badly fumbling fingers I untied his wrists. It was no surprise that he'd already rid himself of the rope around his ankles. I blurted out the story. I watched his eyes get wider and wider.

"This is no joke?"

"Do I look like I'm joking?"

"Let's get Kim."

I handed him a flashlight and we ran down the hall. Our feet sounded heavy on the old rough floorboards. Beams of light swooped and skittered along the walls.

Kim was exactly as I'd left her. Except now she looked scared. I went after the rope around her wrists and Steve freed her legs.

"Jesus! What's going on? It was sort of fun till I heard you guys running around out there..." Her words played out into something like understanding. Her voice went harsh and bloodless. "Where's Casey?"

"Missing."

"What?"

"There's a hole in the wall down there and some kind of tunnel. I found her book bag there. Two of the flashlights were in it. The other was lying in the tunnel. I don't think she left it there on purpose."

She looked at me. I could tell it wasn't registering with her.

"There something in there, Kim. I don't know who or what but something. I think it's got Casey."

She swallowed. "Dan, please don't fool with me."

"I'm not fooling."

"Oh, my god."

"We've got to get help," said Steve.

"No."

I snapped it out at them. The two of them just stared at me. I could feel panic dart suddenly between us like bats in an unfamiliar room. I tried to explain, to keep it under control.

"I don't want to leave her. You understand? It's too late. By the time we got back here, she could be..."

"Wait," said Kim. "Back up a minute. How do you know there's anybody in there?"

"How do I...?"

"Yes! How the hell do you know there's anybody *in there* with her? If she's alone we can just go after her, can't we? If she's just hurt or something?"

"She's not alone, Kim."

"How do you *know*?"

I remembered. And remembering must have showed on me. That feeling of something just out of the reach in the dark. That terrible communication.

"Believe me. I know."

I watched her stare into my eyes and shudder.

"I felt it there, Kim. Very close to me. And it was not like us. It was nothing like you or me at all."

I saw them exchange glances. I knew what they were thinking. If it was as bad as I seemed to think Casey could already be dead. But for me that didn't change a thing. Not as long as I still didn't know.

"I need your help," I said.

"You've got it," said Kim. "But what can we do? We don't have guns. We don't have anything."

"There's stuff in the cellar."

I guess I'd made the rope too tight on her. She rubbed her wrists hard to restore circulation. She winced and looked at Steven.

And for a moment I felt their confusion. Real fear will do that to you—root you dumb and empty to the spot, bankrupt of ideas. I could feel a whirling inside me.

"Look," said Steve finally, "I think you're right. We have to try to find her. But we won't be doing any good going off half-cocked, will we. I mean, what if this is just some elaborate ass-hole practical joke of hers? You know Casey. What if she's just spoofing you? You didn't actually see anything. How can you be sure?"

Try mixing terror and frustration together sometime. You get a fine rage. I felt like I was exploding. My hands were making fists on his shirt collar before I even knew what I was up to.

"You want to see the fucking joke? *You want to see it*? Come on!"

I dragged him to his feet. He didn't fight me. I pushed and dragged him down the hall, anger pouring out of me in huge burly waves. Kim followed, trying to get me off him. She hadn't the muscle for it. When we got to the stairs, I shoved him to one side and marched down in front of them, through the kitchen and down into the cellar.

The anger made me stupid and careless. If anyone had been waiting for us it would have been a very simple matter bringing me down. I was lucky, though. The basement was empty.

I waited for them at the foot of the stairs. I walked them past the piles of storage and threw my beam on the hole in the wall. Seeing it made the fury rumble up again. I grabbed Steve by the back of the neck. I forced him down in front of it.

"*Smell* it," I hissed at him. "Smell it, goddamn you! Inside. That's where I found her bag. She's in there. You think it's fucking funny? You think that's a *joke*?"

I saw something tumble off his cheek.

"Dan, I..."

I let him go. He pulled away. I'd wounded him, all right. I watched him wipe his eyes. I felt great and wonderful. I felt like a damn bully.

Kim moved between us and faced me.

"Are you through now?"

Her voice was ice water. It was good for me and bad too. The shame was as strong as the anger had been. Nothing Steve had said was particularly out of line. It was only reasonable from his point of view. Another time it might have been typically Casey. I couldn't blame him for wanting to believe this was like the others. He hadn't sat in that tunnel like I had. He had no way of knowing.

"Dan...I...I was trying to say..."

"I'm sorry, Steve. I'm just scared, I guess, that's all."

He stopped stammering.

"I was trying to say that I'll help you. Only..."

"Only he's not quite as dumb as you are, Daniel. Suppose you're absolutely right. Suppose there's someone or something in there. Then suppose we go in, and it's something big enough so that three rusty knives can't quite handle it. What happens then? Sorry, Casey? We tried?

"I don't think that's good enough, Daniel. Not good enough for Casey, or for us."

I looked at them. There was no need to apologize further. They knew. They were pretty good people and they knew.

Her voice was calmer now.

"Look," she said. "I could take the car and go for the police. You and Steve could stay here and do whatever you can. I can drive as fast as either of you and I'm a lot more persuasive. But I'm telling you, I don't like the look of that hole. Not one bit. I don't think you should try to go in there."

"We've got to."

"What else can we do?" said Steven.

"Stay here. In case she comes out again. You are not heroes, for christ's sake! I want you to promise me you won't try."

"But what if she..."

"What if she NOTHING! You don't know what's in there; you don't know if the damn thing caved in on her! Jesus! Could we please stop arguing? We're wasting time."

"Okay," I said. "Go."

"Promise me."

Steven hesitated, glanced at me. I nodded.

"I promise," he said. "All right."

"Dan?"

"We'll be here. You know the way all right? You can find the way back to the car?"

"I'm already there."

I put my flashlight beam on the staircase for her and watched her run up the stairs and disappear around the corner through the kitchen. A moment later we heard the front door open and then slam shut again.

The house was silent.

"I'm sorry, Steve. I mean it."

"It's okay. I...care for her too."

We stood there together listening, hoping for sounds behind the wall. Woman sounds. Alive sounds.

There weren't any.

It seemed as though a long time passed. But in the rational part of me I know it wasn't long at all. It was the standing there that made it seem so, listening to our heartbeats pulse down into something a little more like normal, staring into the dark corners of the room, everywhere seeing Casey.

But Kim was as good as her word. In a while we heard the car start up outside and two long blasts on the horn. They sounded very far away to me.

"What are we going to do?" whispered Steve.

"What do you want to do?"

He stared at me a moment and then bared his teeth, the best approximation of a smile he could manage at the time. I gave him one back that had to be just as bad. My guess is we looked like a couple of wolves in feral display.

"I'm not going to like waiting," he said.

"Neither am I."

"It's a half hour into town."

"Twenty minutes if you push it. So what do you think?"

"I think we should have a look inside."

"I was hoping you'd say that."

He shrugged. "I know you were. I'd been very much hoping I wouldn't."

We went through the stuff on the floor.

It was good to do that. It gave you a sense of purpose, of something leading to something, of potency and judgment. We were quiet and thorough and very content to be rooting around in there.

Personally I liked the pitchfork.

There were two tines missing on the left side but the head fit soundly into the shaft, so it didn't wobble, and the shaft was long enough to keep whoever we were liable to meet a good few feet away. Steven found an axe handle. It was sturdy, with about five pounds of weight. The knives were all rusty and useless. We decided to go with what we had.

We stood there looking ready.

We weren't ready.

I knew what he wanted to say to me because I had the same thing to say to him: *are you sure about this?*

Neither of us uttered it.

There was no way to feel good about it, no way at all, but jesus, it was Casey in there, the girl I'd made love to and listened to and watched with growing pleasure for a long time now. The woman who'd told me, finally, some of the reasons for what she was, who saw me as friend and lover. So that the hook was sunk deep. I wasn't about to abandon her.

As for Steve, I suppose he had his reasons too.

I know he did.

I'm trying to explain this now.

Because it wasn't very smart, what we did.

When you're whole and unharmed, no matter how scared you are there's always the feeling that nobody's going to touch you, really. It's only when the pain begins that you realize you're vulnerable. By then it's too late. By then it's a matter of getting out alive, that's all. But before that you jerk yourself off a little. Your mind does a little survey and there you are, strong, intact. So what's to worry? Your body gets insulted: *have I ever let you down in a pinch?* Guess not. And, knees knocking, you plunge right in. Thrilled. Invulnerable. To get strafed by the firepower of your worst nightmares.

People are idiots, basically.

Young people worst of all.

Because kids don't believe in death. They have to be taught in order to believe—and the teacher is always disease or gaping holes in the flesh. Wounds. Pain. That usually comes later in life, but it comes eventually.

All the heroes are children.

So we two, playing with makeshift bats and sharp objects, went inside.

Just a little at first. In that first passageway there was only room to go one at a time, so I led the way, pitchfork always leading me a little, flashlight in my other hand. I could always feel Steven right behind me, crawling up over my ankles half the time, in fact, keeping contact. It felt really good having him there too.

When we turned the corner the passage opened up a bit. But there still wasn't room to go two abreast. So when he started to move up on me I waved him back again. I didn't want to feel cramped in there any more than I had to.

Casey's flashlight was up ahead. I knew when Steven saw it because I heard him groan a little. It sounded very loud in there.

The wind was colder but not so forceful as before. The stink was still bad, though. I wondered what Steve was thinking, encountering it full blast for the first time. I wondered if it was making him sick. You think of weird things at times like that, irrelevant things really, as though your concentration can't handle the sudden strain. I found myself wondering how his whites were holding up. Actually thinking about laundry. It was stunning to me.

I put my flashlight down and tried Casey's. It was dead. I put it in front of my own beam and saw that the clear plastic head was broken, splintered with tiny webbings. Just behind the plastic the aluminum backing was deeply dented in two places roughly opposite one another. As though gripped by a powerful hand or a pair of jaws.

I handed it back to Steve. There wasn't any need to speak. I knew he'd find the same things I had—the dents were impossible to miss. So was their meaning. Somebody had taken the flashlight away from her. And they did not do it gently.

I heard him put it down beside him. I picked up my flashlight and started to move on.

Just ahead a seam of lighter-colored rock caught my eye. Most of what we were crawling through was a grayish black. But this was white. Sandstone or something. Flecked with red. Tiny dots of red no bigger than the head of a pin.

Glistening.

I put my finger to it and it scraped away. It was thick and moist and cold. Blood. I looked closer at the area directly ahead of and to the sides of me.

The wall was sprayed with it. A fine dusting of Casey's blood. Of the life in her.

On the ground, about an inch from my left hand, I saw a small pool of it the size of a quarter.

From now on, I thought, we'd have a trail to follow. *We'd be crawling through Casey's blood.*

Abstract it.

Get it away from you. That's it. Let only the coldness in, the anger.

"What is it?"

"Blood here."

"Oh my god."

"Only a little. Not too bad."

I wouldn't have bought it myself. And neither did he.

"We'll get him, Steve. I'm going to put this pitchfork right up his ass."

We weren't careless. We moved slowly along those fifteen feet or so to that second blind turning, slowly and carefully, under control.

I kept wondering why none of us had heard her scream. It must have happened very quickly. Either that or for some reason it had been impossible to scream. But there should have been something, some warning. I scanned the walls, looking for more blood. There hadn't been enough of it to indicate a neck wound. So what had silenced her?

Why did you come here, Casey? You must have smelled the death inside. I did. How could you have done this to yourself, to me, to all of us?

Nothing you've told me can explain this thing to me. No rape, no seduction, no death, no guilt. You must have known. Suspected at least. Why fling your life around like a pocketful of change? It makes no sense. It never has. It must run very deep, as deep as blood and bone, much deeper than even you knew.

We watched and listened. Even tasted the air I think for some scent of him. But I knew the passageway would be empty. I didn't think I'd be taken unawares. There had been too much connection between us before. In that black war of nerves I had absorbed too deep a sense of him. I'd know when he was near. And this time he'd know I'd come to kill him.

Still I was careful. I knew enough not to trust to sixth senses. I was trusting to care and brains and muscle—and sharp contact. And to Steven too, my backup. Moving along with a will for it behind me.

Look out, I thought.

You've made both of us damned unhappy.

I refused to look for more blood along that track. I tried to push back all thoughts of Casey. I didn't want them weakening me.

I thought I was being very strong and clever.

By the time we reached the end of that section the palms of my hands were dappled red.

The walls opened up into a cavern.

Twenty

THE ROOM WAS CIRCULAR, ROUGHLY, about twelve feet in diameter. Its walls were high, at least fifteen feet or more. In its center lay a wide pool of stagnant water, gray, cloudy-looking. Water bled off the ceiling and dripped back into it—a steady, sharp echo.

The floor was strewn with bones.

Hundreds of them, many cracked and broken.

There were so many it made them hard to identify. Piled, scattered everywhere. I saw fish heads, crab shells, the thin delicate skulls of birds. Others were a whole lot larger. Dogs? Maybe. I remembered that day long ago when we'd peered into the house and watched the carcasses come out one by one. It was possible they were dogs.

It was also possible they were bigger game.

"What is all this?" whispered Steven.

"I don't know."

We stepped carefully into the room. It was a relief to be able to stand upright. A dozen bluebottle flies rose up to greet us. We swatted at them.

I bent down for a closer look. I picked up one of the bigger bones. Something had been at them. There were teeth marks. Something trying to get at the marrow.

I broke one in my hands. It was old and brittle. I felt a measure of relief at that. It was easy to hope they all went back to the days before Ben and Mary abandoned the house—some sort of burial ground for their animals. I didn't want to have to link them with Casey too closely.

We prowled around for a moment or two. The flies got worse. I was looking for traces of blood. There was something odd near the wall to our right. A pile of sticks and twigs pressed flat, covered with a ratty old moth-eaten tartan blanket, half of that covered with dried seaweed and scattered with bones. To me it looked *planned*. Some sort of browse-bed. So there went my burial-ground idea.

Steven was looking at the bones.

"I recognize this one," he said. "It's a cat."

"How do you know?"

"College biology. And there are birds here too, big ones. Gulls, maybe."

"See any dogs?"

My feet crushed tiny bones.

"Maybe. We never took any of those apart. No skulls that I can see. No jawbones."

He sifted through a pile of them near the pool of water. They rattled like pairs of dowels struck together.

"This could be a dog's. Femur. Could very well be."

"See any people?"

In my flashlight beam his face was ashen.

"No people."

"I was thinking Ben and Mary."

"No. No people. Thank god."

I found a thin line of fresh blood beside the pool opposite him, and then a few more drops a couple of feet away. Smeared, as though she'd been dragging. She was bleeding slowly and steadily.

In the cave this deep the flies were not just blue bottles anymore. They were biting. I felt a sharp sting on my cheek, another on my neck. I batted at them to no effect, except to nearly drop the flashlight while its beam jittered wildly across the wet gray ceiling and plunged the area just ahead into darkness.

That scared me.

I didn't want to break any more flashlights.

I controlled myself after that. I put the beam to the walls of the cavern, following the direction of her blood. Then I saw what I was after. Another hole in the wall, just like the one we'd come through.

Steven was slapping at them too by now. They were diving at us both like tiny kamikaze pilots, hitting hard. I slapped at one and felt it smear across my forehead. There was the urge to start swinging with both hands, to drop the pitchfork and run. But that was the edge of panic. And it could kill you.

"Let's get out of here. This way."

Just beyond the entrance the tunnel opened up to roughly the size of a mine shaft. It was good to be able to stand up, even if you had to stoop a little. A whole lot better than crawling.

Good also to be able to go two abreast, to feel the security of another body by your side. To know it sported an axe handle that could bring a man down.

We made good time through there. It was just one long passage with nothing in the distance but rock and more rock as far as you could see. It amazed me, this much tunnel. I guess it started in the seawall and eroded inward. I wondered how many others there were along the coast just like this, maybe even deeper and more extensive.

You could hide forever in a place like this, if you could stand the cold of winter and found some way to scrounge up food and water.

It would never grow warm in here. The rock itself would keep it cool throughout the worst of August, and winter would be pure hell. Whoever had Casey was a thick-skinned sonovabitch, if this was the place he called home.

As I say, it was easy going for a while, with only one direction to go in, but then things got more complicated. The section of tunnel split in two. You could go left or right, and they were about the same in shape and size.

"Shit," said Steven.

"Shit is right."

We looked for traces of blood on the floor. There weren't any—not in either direction. There was no way of telling what that meant for Casey. Maybe the bleeding had stopped because the wound wasn't that bad. On the other hand, dead people stopped bleeding too.

It was bad for us, though. It left us with a choice.

In that place you didn't want choices.

I thought about it for a while.

"Listen," I said. "It seems to me that we've been running parallel to the coastline so far, maybe moving a little inland. That sound right to you?"

"I think so."

"Then I think we should take the right. Seems to me that access to the beachfront would be important to whoever the hell is in here. That hole in the basement can't be his only exit. I'm thinking a hole in the seawall, something like that."

"Some way to collect food and water."

"Right."

"Let's try it."

"I just hope to hell we don't find six more of these. You could get pretty lost in here."

We had lost the flies by now but we still had the stink. As we moved on, though, I started to feel I had it right, because the air seemed fresher, more redolent of the sea.

We were moving through short lengths of passageway—five steps in this direction, ten in the next—but I had the sense that we were basically moving outward toward the rock face. Inside me all the troops were on red alert, armed and watchful. So were Steven's.

Both of us amazed me.

Walking two abreast like that you could feel the pull of tension between us; a strong, supple feeling. Strange. As though we shared the same nervous system, he and I, impulses tugging two sets of muscles, two structures of bone. I hardly knew him, really. But I knew him then.

And you could see why friendships are so easy to come by in combat situations, why the loyalties are fierce ones and why you avoid them if you can, because the trauma runs so deep when shell or bullet shatters them forever. I didn't worry for Steven. I worried for *us*.

We'd reach a corner and wait and listen, holding our flashlights close to the ground. Then we'd throw the beams around the corner and I'd hit the wall opposite us, pitchfork high and ready, while Steve waited to crack somebody's skull with the axe handle.

I think we got the procedure off cop shows.

But it felt good and efficient anyway.

Four times we did this. Each time—nothing.

I was waiting, hoping to feel it like I'd felt it before—that sense of something out there, just out of reach and out of sight. Something big and dangerous waiting for me and ready, just as I was ready for him, this time. I had my backup and my long pointed stick. I was ready.

The hell I was.

I hit the fifth wall. I was sure we were close now.

All the beam showed us was another passageway. Empty, silent.

The corridor was a short one. Six steps maybe. We got halfway down and then stopped. I don't know why we stopped. But again, it was simultaneous. There was a moment there where all we did was look at one another. Eyes like black little beads in our heads.

And I think we *knew*.

Something rough and jagged was happening to my heartbeat. I remember he gave me a little smile. That same curl to the lip as when he was being cute and ironic, only it wasn't that way this time. It was like hello and good-bye all at once.

Just like that.

And between those things lay all life, all time, for both of us.

I turned my light to the ground. The walls loomed with shadows. I stepped into them and threw my beam ahead of me.

And saw what was happening to Casey.

Twenty-one

I HAD A BRIEF IMPRESSION OF A LARGE EMPTY ROOM with high rugged ceilings.

Pillars in the soft rock from roof to floor, pulled thin in the middle like strands of taffy.

Gleaming, dripping.

And Casey.

Propped up against one of them fifteen feet away from us, her bloodied legs spread wide apart, their angle enclosing us within. Her eyes wide, unblinking, flickering like candles in a wind. Seeing her a punch to the solar plexus, a blinding physical shock.

For a moment I simply reeled.

It crouched beside her, its long black bony back to us. I could see its head rise and fall with the lunge of backbone and muzzle and hear the snap of teeth as it worried her.

Her eyes stared through it—through us too—boring back through the tunnel and cellar and house into the woods beyond. At some point she'd put on the army shirt. Now it was torn off completely at the shoulder and dark with blood. There was blood on the blue halter beneath it and more on the cream shorts and across her legs and naked stomach. Her face was very pale.

The huge black dog lunged out of its crouch and snapped at her, very near her face. A sound like the clap of two heavy sticks of hardwood. Her pale blue eyes skittered like trapped birds.

For a moment we froze there.

The sheer awesome size of him was riveting.

I watched the muscles curl and pulse along his back, and he was fascinating as a snake.

He snapped at her again and tore a flap of sleeve off the army shirt as though it were tissue paper. I saw where it had chewed her, dragged her along by the shoulder. The bare white arm looked useless now.

New blood began to well up where there was none before along the side of her upper arm.

He'd taken more than the sleeve.

And I knew where this particular game was going.

I acted. The hero moved.

"Hey!" I said.

It startled even me. The inanity of it. The hoarse echoing loudness of it. *Hey*. Idiotic. But that was what came out. And choked back everything else.

The dog turned.

That is, its head did.

A square black head on a neck as thick as the trunk of a birch tree. I've seen other full-grown dogs that were not as big as that skull was. I felt suddenly very frail.

It moved slowly around and stared at us with cloudy black eyes.

Cataracts, I thought. It's practically blind. An old dog, its black coat flecked with white. And I remembered that among the predators there was nothing more dangerous than the old or sick or blind, because they would hunt anything, even man.

Its muzzle pulled back into a grin that growled like muted thunder. I saw huge curved incisors longer and broader than my thumb, easily three inches long. I saw rows of smaller sharp teeth between them for gripping and pulling, and behind them the blunt wide molars. A grim, discolored killing machine was what I was looking at. Long gray battle scars across the muzzle.

I felt its half-blind stare work its way into me like a burrowing worm, leaving me rubber legged, sweating.

He turned completely.

It was slow and graceful, belying his age. His torso unfolded like the sluice of a great black whip. In full view he was enormous—easily four and a half feet from the tip of the flat black nose to the base of his tail. Standing on his hind legs he'd be seven feet tall, I guessed. As big as a bear.

Of bastard parentage, I think now. Something of the Great Dane about the head. Something of the wolf in the set of the shoulders.

The pitchfork and axe handle seemed like toys.

A pair of tin soldiers was what we were.

No axe handle was going to crack that skull. No ridiculous garden implement was about to pierce that hide. My brain computed the heft and sinew of both of us and compared it with an old sick dog's and we came up looking like sparrows.

I could see the mad strangeness in those eyes.

He could crack us like eggs.

My fear of him was almost superstitious. My voice still echoed in the room.

Hey.

And I thought what if there are more of them?

Beside me Steven went rigid.

It stared at us. Head down, eyes rolled high and moving from one of us to the other. Deciding. Black eyes deciding. A casual, terrible inspection.

And I knew we were no surprise to him. Downwind or not, we'd been expected. He was in no hurry. We were not a problem. It was a matter of who to take down first. He could do it at his leisure.

The animal drooled.

Pleasure. Anticipation.

I'd seen enough dogs to know how it would happen. He'd drop the tense, stiff-legged stance in favor of a very loose, very amiable-looking, very doggy trot. The trot would turn quickly into a deadly lunge of teeth and claws and muscle.

Nice dog. Watch the spume of blood. *Good doggy*.

The only way to go was to move before he did.

I used my smallest voice. "I'm going to move on him," I said.

It took Steven a while to respond. Then he told me okay and I knew he was as ready as he was going to get.

I watched the slow drift of the animal's eyes from Steven back to me. When they returned to Steve again, that would be the time. I'd have to try for the heart. The eyes would ideally be better, or the soft, sensitive nose, but both those targets were too small for me at this distance and I knew how fast and well he'd move them.

I looked down at the massive bony chest and then back to the eyes. I knew where the tines would have to go. I tensed to put them there.

The growl was loud as a buzz saw in that space.

The teeth snapped. Impatience. Display.

And knowledge, too, of what we had in mind.

I know that now.

~~~~~~~~~~

The eyes held on me. Through the cloudy white lenses I sensed a recognition. *Yes, it's me. We've met before. You know me.*

Arrogantly, they shifted.

I rushed him, arms and legs moving like machines in fine order. No missteps. No faltering. My arms drew back the pitchfork and plunged forward with power and accuracy. I surprised myself. I was good. I was very good.

And not nearly good enough.

I was prepared for bone and muscle. There was every bit of me behind it, one hundred seventy pounds. He'd be hard to kill, so it had to be that way—there'd be no second try. So I gave it everything. And felt a sickening scrape along his backbone and a tug of resistance at the hip joint of the right hind leg, and then there was nothing but air.

I fell forward hard, the flashlight skittering out of my hand. I heard it crack and saw it die against one of the vertical columns next to Casey. I still had the pitchfork. I rolled as I fell and hit shoulder-first and kept rolling, over on my back, and pulled the tines up close, expecting to see it looming over me, knowing it would go for the neck.

But it wasn't there.

It was already after Steven.

His flashlight beam slid erratically over the ceiling. I looked up and heard the heavy *thunk* of his axe handle and sighted him in time to watch it bounce off the animal's skull as though it were lightweight plastic.

I heard him wail as the head came up at him and he tried to hit it a second time and it moved so that he overshot his mark, and
~~~~~~~~~~

saw the jaws clamp down on his arm just above the wrist. His scream went higher, shriller. Beneath it the awful crunch of bone as the jaws ground down and through him and the hand crumbled away, falling off his arm, falling slowly like the limb of a tree under a chain saw.

I got to my feet.

Light swung wildly around me as he battered the dog with his flashlight. *His bad hand*, I thought idiotically. I could see the gout of blood pulsing, pouring off his other wrist, the long slash mark on the animal's back where I'd hit him.

I ran toward them, off-balance this time, and reached them just as the flashlight flew out of the bandaged hand in a wide arc and the animal moved again. The light guttered out, clattering against stone, and then went on again, its beam playing over the floor to the right of me. My second stab at him had been in darkness. The pitchfork jarred against solid rock.

When the light went on again there was just a gurgling sound.

Steve was facing me, sitting, his back to the wall beside the entranceway. His eyes were rolled up so only the whites showed. His head lolled off to one side. His mouth was open, and something dark spilled down across his chin.

The dog was at his stomach.

Pulling.

I froze.

The dog's haunches tensed as it tugged again.

He seemed to fold and sigh, his body sliding down the dark wet wall. I smelled urine and feces. In his lap everything turned a ghastly white.

The dog let go. Its jaws continued working something. Its head turned slowly and looked at me.

I backed away.

The animal just stood there, watching me. Its eye catching a beam of light. The room was filled with the stink of us. I backed away further, slowly. There was a column just to the left of me. I wanted to put it between us. I wanted to hide.

I watched his eyes.

My hands clenched the cool moist air.

The animal turned, its old dark body full of luxurious power, and stalked me.

It crossed the beam of light. I saw the tongue slide along its chops. Its mouth was bright with blood. I saw the calm assuredness in every move.

When the easy trot began, I turned and ran.

It was ludicrous, impossible.

Just as impossible not to try.

I ran for the column.

He caught me high on the calf and I went down. The pitchfork tumbled from my hands. I felt the fangs go through me almost painlessly, like razors through soft butter. There was a moment of shrieking terror. Then my head slammed hard against damp, slimy rock. I saw something move far away in front me, against the farthest wall.

I heard laughter. Female laughter.

It was not Casey's. It was old and clogged and choking.

And then I felt nothing at all.

Twenty-two

WHEN I WOKE, THE ROOM WAS RUNNING RED WITH BLOOD.

I lay in a small pool of it. It had run down the side of my head from just above my left ear. It was caked over my eyelids, in my lashes. My vision was a dull red too. That seemed to mean I still had some blood left inside me. That was nice.

The red was flecked with yellow. Starbursts. Tiny explosions. Something huge and awful was gnawing at my leg. I looked down at it. It seemed to contain its own cruel, throbbing heartbeat. A match for the one in my head. I had three heartbeats. Undisputably I was alive then. I had no right to be.

The leg looked wet and terrible.

Thank god for Steven's flashlight, I thought.

I looked around. No black shapes beside me. None anywhere that I could see.

I looked where I thought Steven's body should be. It wasn't there anymore. For a moment I hoped I'd imagined the entire thing. But no.

I looked for Casey. I was disoriented now. I knew she'd been up against one of the columns. Somewhere over there. She ought to have had her back to me. I couldn't see her.

I tried to stand up. It was still too painful and I was much too dizzy. I groaned. It didn't seem to sound as though it came from me. I settled for pushing myself up. Hands to the floor, head dangling. It hurt less that way.

"Dan?"

A tiny voice, coming from a darkened alcove behind me. I tried to turn around.

I heard tears and misery. It was her voice, but changed somehow. I could almost smell the tears, their salt humidity. I got out the name, a whisper.

"Casey."

It made me feel much better. We were both alive in there.

"You all right, Case?"

She shuffled out of the shadows, her face very pale. The naked right arm hung at her side like a dead thing. With an effort I turned to her. She stumbled to her knees in front of me.

"It…it hurt me." Sobbing. No sound. Just the involuntary shuddering of her body.

My leg howled as I turned on it further, reaching out to her.

"Hurt me bad."

"I know. It's all right, Case. It's all right."

It wasn't, though. I held her and looked over her shoulder for the pitchfork. It was there just beyond us, tines curved upward.

She'd never felt so good to me.

"I did this," she said. "I did this to you."

"No."

It was a useless lie.

"I saw Steven..."

She broke. Her body trembled. She was cold to the touch, and I could feel the hard, bunched-up muscles beneath her clothing.

When the tears were under control again she sat pressed to me tightly, face gleaming. She looked up at me. The fathomless blue eyes were wide and liquid. They reminded me of that other night not long ago. I knew she was mourning Steven. There was no help for it. I seemed to see down into the suddenly grown-up heart of her. I saw fear and compassion, and great hurt.

"You found me."

"We did."

It all came pouring out then, how she'd sat in that first passageway waiting for me, ready to turn her flashlight beam to my face and scare hell out of me, so that her back was toward it when it found her and took her down by the shoulder, a powerful, brutal black shadow in the midst of shadows.

"I couldn't even scream for you," she said. "I wanted to. God knows I wanted to. But all I could do was fight. All I could do was push at him and try...try to...and then soon I couldn't even do that anymore. I gave up, I guess, and he started...dragging me...along...and all I could do was lie there and stare at him weak as a baby. And then I felt something hot, hot and red like it was throughout my whole body, and I guess I passed out then. All I remember after that is something like pressure waking me, pressure in my shoulder. And there he was, snapping at me, just inches from my face...snapping. That sound!"

"Where is it now?" I asked her. "Did you see?"

"They...took him...through there."

She pointed toward the far wall. There was another opening there.

"I think that's where it opens to the sea. When I was lying there, I could smell it."

"*They*?"

I remembered the cold hoarse laughter.

"Is it Mary, Case?"

"It's both of them. At least I think it is. I've been...in and out a lot. But there's a woman, and there's a man. Who else could it be?"

"Ben and Mary Crouch. Jesus."

"They're horrible, Dan. And that thing. I saw Steven. It picked him up and dragged him...like a doll. And parts of him...parts of him were trailing..."

"Don't."

"...were spilling out of him, trailing along the floor..."

"Stop it, Case!"

She looked at me. It was horror and not loss of blood that had bled her white. In her eyes was a surfeit of horror.

The death freak in her was dead and I'd never miss it. Instead there was sadness now and a grim responsibility—to me, to what Steven had tried to do for her, to herself. I saw that as I watched her pull herself together. She was finished with the past. I looked into her eyes and tried to pour out hope to her through mine, a hope I barely felt, a strength I could only command by forgetting where we were and how we came to be there.

So that suddenly I was the cynic. Not her.

She tried to smile. For a brave second she succeeded. And I could have cried for the joy of it. Because the bravado was gone. I saw the courage suddenly flare up in her again and it was pure and undiluted, the very best of her, and in that moment she handed it to me.

"Where's Kim?"

"The police. She took the car."

She nodded. "Can you walk?"

"I think so."

"Try."

She stood up, and I got on my hands and knees and then reached for her good shoulder. I hauled myself up. I put some weight on the leg. From knee to ankle something stretched and screamed at me. But it held. "Okay," I said.

I reached for the pitchfork and the pain raced up my leg and right up through the shoulders. I damn near fainted. I was still making mistakes. She put out her hand to steady me. In a moment the pain was down to something bearable. She handed me the pitchfork. One-handed.

"Wonder why they left it?"

"I think your friend Rafferty was right," she said. "I think they're stupid. They don't count on much from us. Not wounded."

"You think that makes them stupid?"

"Yes, I do."

I was almost able to smile.

"That shoulder looks bad."

It wasn't just the shoulder. The upper arm too was mauled and bloody.

"I can't feel much. I think he did something to the nerves. But I can't move it, Dan."

"Don't try. Let's just get out of here." I listened. "All three of them went through there?"

"No. The woman and the dog. The man—Ben—I don't know where he is." She frowned and shook her head. "I think I remember...I think he went back toward the house. I'm not sure."

"Think. It's important.

"Oh god."

"Come on, Case."

"Okay. Yes. All right. I remember a shadow. Movement. Yes. He's back there, Dan."

"Shit. Checking to see if there are more of us, probably. That means we're screwed either way."

"And he's big. Very big."

"Great. Wonderful. Okay, let's work this through. It's a long way back there, and a lot of it's narrow tunnel. We'd have Ben ahead of us for sure. And if they come back looking for us, we'd have Mary and that thing behind us too. With no room to turn around, maybe. I can't say I like that much."

"But the dog, Dan."

"We don't know what the hell's in that direction, except the sea is there somewhere..."

"Pretty close, I think."

"And Mary and the dog are there too, somewhere. What do you like?"

"Dan?"

"What."

She hesitated. "I was about to say I loved you. But what if I'm just grateful? Very grateful."

"I'll take it. Either way."

"You will, won't you."

"Yes."

She moved quietly to the flashlight and picked it up and then returned to me. She looked at me a moment.

"It's love," she said. "It always was, I think."

"I know. For me too, Case."

We stood there, not even touching.

What a terrible time to find out how good life can be, I thought. And how good to find out anyway.

We let the moment plant its seed deep, knowing there might never be a harvest. Her smile was a little rueful, but mostly it was glad. She came slowly, gently into my arms.

"I never want to see that dog again," she said, "but I'll take what we don't know over what we do."

"Same old Casey."

I held her close and then released her. There was almost a pain, a physical pain, at the parting.

I took the flashlight from her and located Steven's axe handle in the beam. Without a word she picked it up. Then we turned and touched hands and slowly we moved on.

We had not been the first to come through there.

They lay waiting for us in the passageway. A pair of human

skeletons, rags falling away to scraps over cracked broken bones, lying in the dark.

Whether the dog had killed them or had only gotten to them after death we couldn't tell. But it was easy to see where the bones had been scraped and gnawed. On one of them the legs had been separated from the torso and dragged a few feet away. The shinbone on the left leg was gnawed clear through. It was splintered like a piece of green wood. The skulls bore teeth marks too.

I'm told the brain is a choice morsel.

So Ben and Mary had finally yielded up their secrets, some of them. Fled with a pet or two. One of whom had grown very big and very old and had tasted human flesh.

Fled through a hole in the wall. Used it, probably, to gather up supplies now and then. And when it was sealed up, cut it open again.

They had lived like animals here. It was easy to imagine a life of scrounging, gathering, hiding. Scavenging the beaches. At night perhaps, the ghost crabs scurrying sideways underfoot, pale as wax in the light of the moon. A captured gull's nest. Hidden traps along the shoreline. A stray cat. A stray dog. And always, hiding. The world outside the proven implacable enemy. Their entire army a pair of black, powerful jaws.

The skeletons were somewhat on the small side. One of them in scraps of denim.

Kids, probably. No older than us, and maybe younger.

Kids again.

I wondered if dog or man or woman had killed them. I wondered if they'd fought and lost and died as Steven had. I felt very, very vulnerable.

The corridor was a short one. Casey was right—from here you could smell the sea. You could hear it too, the faint easy brushstrokes of dead low tide. To me it sounded like freedom.

You couldn't help but reconsider going back the way we came, Ben or no. Not after those corpses. But in the passageway we'd be much more open to attack. Besides, I wasn't wholly sure of the way. I could see us missing a turn, the panic, the fear that they could be in front of us or behind, the impossibility of covering ourselves with only one light between us. They knew these tunnels. We didn't.

No, the way out was ahead of us. Past them. Through them.

Close by.

We moved toward the hiss of the sea. Its sound was seductive, dangerous. It could excite you, give you hope. And it could mask other sounds.

Fight the sound, I thought.

I saw a thin streak of moonlight filter through the passage. We were close now. It gave me an idea. A way to increase our odds a little. I pulled her near me and whispered.

"Douse the light."

She understood immediately. We stood silent in the darkness waiting for our eyes to adjust to the dim light. The dog and Mary Crouch would be ahead of us. In moonlight. When we faced them there would be a moment when we'd see them better than they'd see us. And that was our moment.

"Take her," I said.

She turned her head and nodded. We rounded the corner.

The room was small, maybe fifteen feet in diameter, with low ceilings. Once the tides had come through here. The floor was covered with round stones polished smooth. Directly ahead of us was an opening four feet wide by six feet high. There were three browse-beds arranged perpendicular to the opening. I could picture them lying there on warm summer nights like this one, the dog's keen nose facing the opening. Outside we could see the blue-black of night and the stars. A clean sudden peace.

Before us, the dog. The nightmare.

Feeding.

A glance at Steven was all I could handle and all I could spare. It could freeze you, slide you into madness. And the dog was busy now, its muzzle ferreting through blood and bone, its senses not quite so alert.

He was facing the stars.

I heard the crack of bone. The muzzle rose in profile and I saw the froth and drool, the mad stare in one blind eye. It dipped back down into the kill.

And there was Mary too.

An old gaunt woman in rags, her thin wiry back hunched and studded with backbone like scars on the trunk of a tree. Her hair a fright wig of dirty matted gray and white. The long musculature of her arms taut as cables.

I heard her voice crooning to the dog as she knelt beside it and stroked the black expanse of its body from neck to haunches, a soft, high, even tone of pleasure and serenity tossed in the gentle wind that brushed through the entrance to the cave, while the dog tore and broke and violated the empty ruins of my friend.

Her hand moved like a claw over its body. Lovingly. And wordlessly she sang to him, urging him on, like a mother to a baby. Like a lover.

I felt my face contorting, my stomach heave. I wrenched my eyes away from her.

I looked at the dog.

And realized there was no clear line of attack.

For targets the pitchfork had only its back and hindquarters. I could do him no real damage there. I needed the breast or muzzle. I felt a moment of frustrated panic. Soon one of them would sense us behind them, and then I'd have my shot. But the dog would be moving. Fast and deadly.

I fought for control.

I felt Casey stiffen beside me. The fear was coming back to her now, rising off me, infecting her. I had only seconds before we'd both be useless for anything but a blind run, and there was no running from that monster. From the woman maybe. But not from him.

To my left was a large round stone. One long step away.

I handed her the pitchfork. I saw a moment of confusion on her face and then I saw she trusted me. She winced as she tucked the axe handle under her wounded arm. We were too close to them to let it fall. She hefted the pitchfork and braced the handle under her shoulder, pointing it toward him, holding it like a lance. I listened for the sounds its jaws made, the scrape of teeth against bone. I remembered counting in the dark, how hard it was to hear over the internal sounds. It would be the same for them. That would cover me.

I heard what I wanted to hear and took the step.

The stone was heavy, wet and slimy on the bottom. My leg tore painfully as I bent to lift it. But the weight felt good in my hands.

I was lucky. The rock was standing free of other stones and lifting it hadn't made a sound. The animal feasted on, oblivious to everything but the blood smell and the eating sounds, nearly sated with pleasure. The woman crooned and stroked, smoothing the short thick hair that gleamed in the light of the moon.

I guess I'd pictured leaning over him and crushing his skull. But that was impossible. I could risk another step toward him. There were too many stones between me and him to warn him. He was four-and-a-half feet long. I wasn't even sure I could throw the rock that far, much less hope to hit his skull with any accuracy.

He stood straight legged on all fours, legs splayed slightly, neck and head down, back arched. I studied him. The back was vulnerable. Not to pitchforks, but to weight.

So I knew what I had to do.

I didn't even breathe.

I was a million years old. A caveman in the moonlight.

I raised it. It must have weighed thirty-five pounds. I pulled together every inch of muscle. I arched my back and bent my arms at the elbow and then snapped forward—the rock and me with it.

The rock arced down.

It looked right.

I wondered if I'd catch Mary's hand in there.

I hit the bad leg much too hard. I stumbled, fell.

There was a snapping sound like rock against rock and I felt a sudden rush of despair. I heard Casey call my name. I hit solidly with both hands in front of me. Something roared beside me. I felt the heat of its body terribly near my face and head, smelled its raw moist breath.

I rolled over. Stones bruised my back and thighs. Suddenly I was staring into the enormous snapping mouth only inches away, spraying me with spittle, sounds like shots from a pistol—and beneath it, that immense ungodly roar. Casey screamed and the head jerked away from me.

She'd used the pitchfork.

Two of the tines had entered its neck at the shoulder. She was strong and she'd sunk them deep.

The body whipped around.

I saw where the rock had hit him. His back legs were dragging, as useless as Casey's arm. I felt a saving flush of pleasure. We'd broken him, skewered him. Casey held on.

The woman was on her feet and moving toward them.

I lunged at her, grabbed her by the legs and pulled her down. The legs felt scaly in my hands, dry as leather. The woman whirled and shrieked at me, pounding me with her hands. I saw her face. Eyes dark and glittering. A crone's face, a Halloween mask, pointed, webbed and shrill. Waves of foam spilling out of her toothless mouth, over her chin. Her breath a reek of corpses.

Beside me the dog whipped side to side. And still Casey held the pitchfork, leaning her weight into the handle, sinking it deeper.

Leaning in too far.

The dog screamed, dug in with his front paws and heaved. His shoulder muscles rippled, his eyes tossed and rolled. I knew what he was going to do. It was impossible but I saw it coming. I tried to warn her.

"Casey! Drop it!"

I reached for a rock. I pulled myself up over the woman until I straddled her. Brittle claws broke off along my cheek. I felt the blood well up. I saw her dark eyes close a split second before I hit her. The nose broke open. The cheekbones fell away to a strange, sunken angle. The legs kicked and trembled.

I looked up.

The dog heaved.

The muscles in his neck were thick and hard as rigging. The pain must have been amazing but there was nothing in him but a crazy meanness now. I could see Casey's grip faltering on the pitchfork. The dog lurched toward her, sinking it deeper. He got it into him good and solid and then he jerked it away from her as though she were a child in a bad match of tug-of-war.

He got free of her.

And then he hauled himself toward her.

At her. A fast, drunken lunge. While she struggled for balance.

I was on my feet, trying to get to him on the other side, to the handle of the pitchfork, to push it so far into him that it would stop him. It quivered like a bowstring. My foot slowed me down.

Just enough.

I had my hands on the handle as he went for her again and even the crippled arm worked somehow as she tried to fend him off, the immense heavy bulk of him that tore up high into her neck below the chin and ripped her apart and covered them both with a shower of bright blood.

I screamed.

The animal pulled her down, its right front paw tearing four long gashes from the base of her neck to her stomach.

I don't even think she felt them.

But I did.

I had the handle by then. I had it and I used it. I was screeching with rage and pain and I pushed, screamed and pushed with all my strength, the image of her open mouth and eyes searing into my brain. The animal let go of her and tried to shake me, just as it had done to her. It thrashed at me. Snapped. Pulled. But I was crazy then, and I was using two good hands instead of one and I stayed on, riding him on the end of a long sharp stick, pressing it deeper with a power I never knew I had, riding him down into the night.

There was blood rolling off his shoulder and I saw it change suddenly from a dark ooze to a bright arterial spray. And then he was more than even my rage and hatred could contain.

He hit one side of the cave and then the other. The mouth foamed and spilled. The useless hind legs began to twitch. Its howling chilled me to the bone.

A moment later the massive head turned upward one last time. The mouth opened and closed as though baying at the far unseen moon. Its head moved slowly down. Its cloudy eyes froze like small round stones.

I went to Casey.

I had to crawl. My body was trembling with exhaustion and something else, something close to shock. I felt myself moving in and out of reality as though a drug were working in me. I would see her there just beyond me, blue eyes open wide, lips parted. I'd see the tides of red sliding over her body. And then she'd be alive and laughing at me across a long white beach, she'd be upstairs in my apartment walking slowly toward me, I'd touch her, smell her hair, her skin.

I'd feel the seaworn stones beneath my hands and knees and that would bring me back. I didn't want to come back. I moved toward her. It was slow and hard, like moving through deep water.

I had nearly reached her when I saw him standing there.

Ben Crouch.

He was tall, hard, powerful. His hair was long and matted as Mary's had been. His beard was sparse, long in patches, almost nonexistent elsewhere. The clothes were filthy rags, shapeless, torn. His arms were bare. The muscles in them bunched and shifted as he clenched his long yellow fingers into fists. I felt the strength of him. It was like being in the presence of the dog again. It pulsed off him in angry waves and crashed like breakers against the walls of the cave. His small dark eyes played slowly across the room, over all of us there, and then came to rest on me.

Casey's axe handle lay at his feet. He stooped slowly to pick it up. His gaze never left me.

I had expected to see imbecility in his eyes. It wasn't there. I felt him measuring me. His mouth was set in a thin taut line. Rafferty was wrong. All of us were wrong. It was no idiot standing there. He was far more dangerous than that.

On the axe handle his grip had turned the knuckles white.

I filled each hand with a stone. Puny things to use against him. My strength had not returned to me. I waited.

He looked at Casey.

Then at the dog.

Then at Mary. He looked at her for a long time.

And then his eyes returned to me.

As I say, my mind was not quite working right just then.

And I'm not sure it is at all possible to see your own face reflected in the face of another. I've already told you that there was a feeling of being drugged by then. But that's what I seemed to see there. My own face. Me in him. The same loss. The same fear and frustration and anger. And finally, the same mute empty resignation.

My stomach rolled, my head tumbled. I closed my eyes for a moment.

When I opened them, he was gone.

Twenty-three

THEY FOUND US ON THE PEBBLE BEACH.

They thought we both were dead, because I wasn't responding to much by then. We were lying together, and I guess

I'd arranged her arms around me somehow. A lot of that's missing, and I don't necessarily want it back.

I wonder how I got her down there.

I never could have carried her, not with my leg the way it was. So I supposed I dragged her down, just to get us out of there. But I don't remember that either.

I have no idea how long we waited.

There were two parties, one that came through the tunnel like we had, another searching along the beach. I'm told they arrived at nearly the same time, the second group a bit behind the first. Kim was with the second party. They wouldn't let her go in through the wall.

She says that the first she saw of me was one of the policemen wrapping me in a blanket. There was a second blanket covering Casey. I was glad she hadn't seen her. Gladder still that she hadn't seen Steven. She'd pointed out the entrance to them, and that was all. They said it was possibly dangerous.

Days later, we almost laughed at that.

I was sedated, hospitalized, treated for the leg wound and assorted cuts and bruises.

My parents came to visit, and they each had the good grace not to mention how stupid it all had been. My mother thanked god a lot. She seemed nervous all the time and astonished that I'd lived. My father always seemed to carry a kind of hearty seriousness about him around me, as though we were both somehow transported back to World War II and I was his bunkmate, who'd had the bad fortune to get himself shot but who would doubtlessly recover. Strangely, I appreciated that.

Rafferty came by.

It was awkward. About all he could do was tell me how sorry he was and shake his head in wonderment. I think he felt a little responsible. As though it all went back to that day we went through the garbage cans together. I tried to reassure him. Though maybe, in a way, it did.

I learned from Rafferty that all they'd ever found of Ben Crouch was a set of footprints leading down the beach which stopped in the dark wet sand at the tide line. Drowned? Everyone seemed to think so. I hoped not. I sincerely hoped not.

And still do.

Kim was there constantly. "When you're up to it," she said, "I want to know how it was. Not now, but sometime."

She never mentioned it after that. She'd just sit long hours holding my hand and watching me stare off into space, into blue eyes and sunlight, and she didn't disturb me and didn't need to talk. I appreciated that most of all.

Once I was out I saw a lot of Kim. My mother once hinted that she thought it might turn into something. It did, but not the way she was thinking. It became a friendship, and a strong one—one I maintain to this day with letters and phone calls. She's five hundred miles away now. Her husband understands.

One afternoon toward the end of August, I made good on my promise to tell her what went on in there. It was rough on both of us but worth it. We sat in Harmon's for a long time afterward, sipping cokes, saying nothing.

By then I knew I was leaving town, going to Boston. I had a job there that my dad had arranged for me, and I was hoping a small Beacon Hill school was going to accept me for the fall term. As it turned out I did get in. Just barely. She was returning to Chestnut Hill. There was no staying in Dead River after what happened. Not for either of us.

Kim never saw the town again.

I went home now and then to visit my folks. But it was never good for me. It was strictly duty.

Anyway, we sat there a long time while hamburgers slid in and out of the microwave and sodas were poured and people came and went, and I got to thinking about Casey and that last time we'd had together when she'd said she loved me, and how changed she was by then. I knew it was finally clear to her as it was to me that the end of all the useless risk was not thrills but waste and death, a death from within—and that our being in love had finally repudiated all that, and we were strangely happy. In the midst of all the terror, we were happy. The caves had shown us the worst the world could do to you, and for just a moment, something of the best.

I was going to Boston because I wasn't dying anymore. Inside, I felt cleaner than I'd ever been.

I tried to explain that to Kim.

"You've got a second chance," she said. "Me too. So do I." Then she shook her head. "Steve and Casey—they were both so *good* at the end."

It's odd how things come around.

A year ago last December I drove by the Crouch place and there was smoke coming out of the chimney. Someone was living there. I wondered if they knew. I asked Rafferty.

"Sure, they know. Everybody does. But the guy living there is just a caretaker. He'll be there two or three months, tops, while the surveyors and execs do their work. You know who owns that property now? Central Maine Power. The town bought it from the bank just like everybody wanted them to do for Ben and Mary. Then CMP bought it from the town. Scuttlebutt is that what we're going to have there is a waste dump from the nuclear plant in Wiscassett. Ain't that a killer? Nobody knows for sure, of course. But god knows it would be just like the town fathers. Bring some industry into town. Some jobs. And of course, ten years down the road you kill the fish."

He paid some serious attention to his beer.

"That house is well over a hundred years old, you know."

I'm thirty-five this coming November.

Basically, college paid off pretty well for me.

I'm employed.

I live in Manhattan.

I think of Casey.

I can't say I've been in love that way since. Not once. But then I never really expected to be. I think of her often, and sometimes it seems that everything I do is just a substitute for having her there.

Sometimes.

Because the woman I live with I'm close to.

She is switching careers at thirty-seven. And I'm writing this.

It's no big thing, but both of us have our little risks.

Risky Living: A Memoir

By Jack Ketchum

1. There's A Wheel In My Hand But I Can't Steer

The first real love of my life was hooked on speed. She mainlined crystal meth.

1967 was a long time ago so I don't recall exactly how we met. She was a student at Emerson in Boston—a sophomore to my junior when she started shooting the stuff—so I'd hazed her the year before. I'm sure I met her then but the specific circumstances elude me.

Remember hazing?

The thinking was this. You put a new class of kids through a week of pure hell. You're a sophomore and they're lowly freshmen so they're at your bidding. You went through the same thing the year before but now it's your turn. They tote and fetch for you. They go down for pushups or sit-ups or run in place. You make them eat mysterious "desserts" —like mango chutney straight from the jar. You call them names. They call you sir or ma'am. You can do practically anything to these kids except physically push them around or make them late for class.

Sooner or later they gather together. There's talk of rebellion. Hell, their parents are *paying* for this shit! Leaders emerge. Bonds form. Plans are made and discarded. Clear-headed "advisors" from the junior class, who are otherwise not involved in all this, urge them to keep the peace.

Hell Night rolls around finally and you herd them into an auditorium and wander amidst them for a half hour while the abuse flows like poison. Groans and screeches and harsh metal discord issue from the sound system. Lights are low. Then gone altogether, replaced by flashlights darting into freshman faces. They're screaming, yelling. *You're* screaming and yelling even louder. All hell's about to break loose in there.

The stage lights rise to dim. One of their leaders is there. Blindfolded, tied up hand and foot. Then what *isn't* supposed to happen, happens. Suddenly the guy's getting the living shit beat out of him. It looks absolutely real! He's in on it of course but the crowd doesn't know that yet and just before they rush the stage and punches start to fly the house lights come up and the whole sophomore class is grinning and applauding and embracing the enemy. Welcome! You're one of us! Aren't you *happy*?

The weird thing was that for most of us this actually worked. It had for me the year before. I'd emerged as one of the angriest of the whole damn class, then afterward embraced the ruse wholeheartedly. And this year—perhaps because of that—I was class President. So that along with the Hazing Master and Hazing Mistress I was god to these kids.

I loved the part. I played it half Dracula and half Wolfman. Alternately quiet slinking evil and utterly ravenous.

The following year when Jen—I'll call her Jen—moved into the basement apartment below my own third-floor apartment she told me that at first she was actually afraid of me.

A few months later she was scaring *me* on a daily basis.

Taking risks.

2. I Don't Believe In Omens, But I Think You Can Know When You're In Trouble.

Jen was the first to turn me on to marijuana. She and her girlfriend and I smoked a joint in my apartment and then in the midst of this strange new sensation which was nothing like the beer-highs I'd been used to and under the influence of which I felt at once elated and confused somebody decided it would be a good idea to take a walk. Nice night.

I no sooner hit the streets of Beacon Hill when paranoia descended like an oncoming Angus bull. Streetlights seemed more like spotlights, preternaturally bright. The distance between my feet and my eyes was way too far—as though I was walking with somebody else's feet. Every passing car was brimming with cops.

The girls were used to getting high of course so they went their merry way chattering about whatever while I shambled along behind them in the grip of something very much like existential terror. Even their chattering frightened me.

How could they be so normal? *Had they actually* smoked *that joint? Had they maybe poisoned me? Revenge for the goddamn hazing?*

When they turned into an alley—an *alley* for godsakes! — that connected West Cedar Street to Charles Street without saying a word to them I hightailed it back home to my apartment. With the door locked behind me I felt safe again. At least I did initially. Then I thought, what if they come back looking for me? I bet they will. I'd been a total coward, that was clear enough. And I already had the beginnings of a major thing for Jen. What in the world was I thinking? What would *she* think of *me*?

More paranoia.

My solution to the problem was to turn off all the lights and sit huddled in the dark of my living room. Nobody home.

And after a while I heard a knock at the door and Jen and her girlfriend calling me and more knocking and then a kind of puzzled laughter as they drifted away downstairs.

The next day I told her I'd missed their turn into that alley somehow and wandered the streets of Boston for an hour or so looking for them.

She laughed. More importantly, she bought it.

I smoked a lot of dope with her after that mostly down in her apartment and gradually we became lovers of sorts.

I say *of sorts* because her first love was speed. I learned that early on.

3. But Right Away She Scared Me

She'd go into the bathroom and come out a different version of herself suddenly all bright and cheerful when moments before she'd been depressed as hell talking about her troubled relationship with her father back in New Jersey and all the shit that was going to hit the fan once her mom and dad discovered she'd dropped out of college or the break with her former boyfriend or whatever, but she'd be moving around the apartment now like a woman with a mission—*cleaning*, my god, I remember her cleaning practically every surface of the place over and over—switching cuts on the record player and talking about the songs, the records, the Beatles' lyrics or Donovan, searching out books on her bookshelf to reference this point or that or else poems by Rilke or Baudelaire or Rimbeud to read to me and this could go on all night and well into the mornings and usually did.

When she confessed to me the source of all this energy I wasn't that surprised. I'd already tried the occasional Dexedrine to finish up a paper here and there. Even the occasional Black Beauty. It was only that she was *shooting*. It was the needle I was scared of. What if she overdosed? What if some innocent air-bubble in the works exploded in her brain?

Whenever she'd disappear into the bathroom I was afraid it was for the last time. Afraid I was never going to see her again.

Not alive anyway.

To try to keep up with her jagging I started snorting the stuff myself. I was holding tight to my class-schedule but weekends we'd go without any sleep at all and the crash after two nights running and living on nothing more than OJ to keep up the good old Vitamin C was brutal.

And in the end I *couldn't* keep up with her. Not if I wanted to stay in school. She'd already rejected that option.

So had most of her friends, none of whom I liked or trusted. But while I was hanging in there attending to classes she'd be gone with them for days on end. To god knows where. Cambridge maybe. Some crash-pad way up on the Hill. You never knew. There were days and nights I literally waited by the phone for a call which never came unless she'd arrived back home again. There were fights. Recriminations. I felt I had a right to know where she was at least—and even who she was with. We loved one another, didn't we? *Well, then?*

Beneath it all was the fear of that goddamn needle. Fear that it would get to her sooner or later. That it almost had to.

There was a saying, rightly or wrongly attributed to William S. Burroughs. *There are old junkies. But no old speed-freaks.*

I'd heard it many times.

4. That Night We Slept Together On My Bed. In the Morning She Was Gone...

Did we make love? Of course we did—though not very well. Speed is the natural enemy of orgasms. Or as she told me, shooting speed was a powerful orgasm in itself and the real thing just didn't compare. But I loved her body—her generous mouth, the softness of her skin. I loved simply holding her. And I held her a lot. The downslope of Jen's high after two or three nights of riding it and despite the grass or downers we used as buffers as often as not was a case of total emotional meltdown. The sadness in her seeping through like some slow quiet flood of dark water. I remember holding onto her until her body gave in and the shakes stopped and finally she slept. They say that the sense of taste is the most powerful agent of memory. I believe I can still recall the taste of her tears.

5. "What Do You Want, Case? What's Worth Having?"

I did a terrible thing.

I got her a kitten.

I believe I was a little insane by then because I damn well should have known. She was already much too thin. Her jaunts into the Boston wilderness had gotten longer and longer. Each crash harder. But I thought, what she maybe needs is some responsibility here, a really good reason to live and do so somewhat normally, someone or something to give her full-time love to. I knew she was very much capable of love.

I knew she loved cats. So I went to the ASPCA. I went to the market on Charles Street and bought cat food and a cat box and litter. Then the kitten and I—a tiny black and white tuxedo—waited in my apartment for the phone call that would tell me that she finally had returned to hers. And while I petted and scratched him and he purred against my chest I instructed him in his duties. *Out loud*. Through tears of what seemed to me hope and joy at the time but were probably more like desperation.. *He was to purr a whole lot just like he was doing right now. He was to sleep with her every night. He was to be good and sweet and love her like crazy*.

When the phone call came I slipped him into the pocket of my coat and went downstairs and from the look on her face when I presented him to her I knew I'd done the right thing. She adored him immediately. Couldn't believe I'd done this for her. We found makeshift toys for him and played well into the night. There is nothing quite so beguilingly ridiculous as a kitten playing in a new environment and the night was simply lovely.

What'll we call him? she wondered. Jen was very fond of Kenneth Patchen, THE JOURNAL OF ALBION MOONLIGHT in particular. A book at once lyrical and drenched in a sense of loss and fear and suffering.

Had I not been so happy for all three of us I might have seen it right there.

Albion, she said. *We'll call him Albion.*

I don't think it was a month later that Albion was gone. Jen was as devastated as I'd ever seen her.

She'd taken her kitten with her one night to show to some friends.

She didn't remember where.

6. There Was No Way To Feel Good About It, No Way At All...

"Come here. I want you to see it," she said. "Then maybe you won't be so goddamn *scared* all the time."

Or something to that effect.

She was in the bathroom and this time the door was wide open.

We'd been having a fight. I'd begged her to cut it out, to get help. Probably for the hundredth time. *I'm doing what I do for godsakes—I'm shooting up and then I'm going out. No you're not. Yes I am.*

And this time I was just mad enough to say all right, fuck it. So I stood in the doorway and watched her tie off. Use the dropper and the spoon and the match, use the needle. Almost a cruelty about her now, a kind of awful pragmatism, as though she were saying to me, this is the real world, asshole, my world—the one you're too damn chickenshit to watch. Well, watch it now. Watch me swoon.

So I did.

If my saying *I don't remember exactly* seems almost like a motif here it's important to imagine the changes I'd been through—the changes and the times. In the course of a single year I'd gone from Class President, who you could often catch in suit and tie, to tie-dye longhaired hippie. Elvis had been replaced in my affections by the Beatles and the Byrds and the Stones. Not only was I snorting meth and smoking dope and hash but I was tripping on acid and mescaline too.

So I really *don't remember exactly* what prompted me to call Jen's sister.

I know that by then it was not only a case of my fearing the needle but fearing for her mind and body as well. You rarely bothered to eat on speed—it seemed irrelevant—so that over the past few months she'd gotten so damn skinny that her breasts were disappearing and her skin stretched tight over her hips and ribs. Her color was gone. Her eyes were bruised from lack of sleep. Her memory was shot. Her crashes got so bad and so prolonged that I feared for the strength of her heart.

Her family knew nothing of this. The one thing she was always dutiful about were her calls to mom and dad and she'd skipped coming home on *school vacations*. They didn't seem to mind or worry. They trusted her.

So as I say, I don't know exactly what incident prompted it. Or if there was any incident at all but merely a desperate cumulative exhaustion of the spirit.

But I called her sister and turned her in.

Tell your parents, I told her. Tell them to come get your sister.

I think she's dying.

It was not easy to make this call because it was going to be the end of us, of Jen and me. Jen would not forgive this phone call. How could she? I was betraying her deepest secret, revealing her naked in deepest pain. It was going to throw not only her but her entire family into a world of grief.

I wasn't kidding myself. I knew that part of this was also a matter of self-preservation. If possibly I was saving her life here then I was trying to save my own life too. I'd carry more than a little guilt around for this. But I could not any longer bear the constant ache and sorrow of loving someone who seemed not to love herself.

I could only hope that in time she'd forgive me.

In time she did. But it was the end of us all the same.

7. THE DEATH FREAK IN HER WAS DEAD…

Therapy worked its slow and agonizing wonders.

Jen married, had a child. Divorced and married again.

The last time I heard from her she seemed happy.

A strange link between us remained over many years. Now and then I'd call her. Not on birthdays or holidays but always just out of the blue. She'd invariably tell me that it was uncanny. That whenever I called she'd been down and depressed. As though I somehow sensed over great distances that she needed to talk with me and only me at exactly that time and that our talks always served to soothe her.

8. …AND I'D NEVER MISS IT.

We lost touch years ago. I have no idea where she is now and we have no friends in common of whom I might ask.

So wherever you are, Jen, I hope you're well and peaceful. And forgive me again. This is merely a poor sketch of you and by no means does you justice.

I'll never miss the risks you took with your life or those we took together. But you always miss the ones you love, don't you. I think you must. Alive or dead, happy or troubled. It's a human imperative I think. Something which fades only when you fade.

And sometimes with great good luck it even lives awhile further, in between the lines, in the pages of a small book.

—Jack Ketchum
June, 2007